Escape from the Casa Grande

Josh Martin has headed west seeking adventure. He finds it – and also finds a life and death situation, becoming marooned in a lonely, desolate valley with no hope of remaining alive unless he can employ the few skills that he possesses.

To add to his problems, he also has to care for Ellie, a girl who is the sole survivor of an Apache raid.

Escape from the Casa Grande

P.J. Gallagher

A Black Horse Western

ROBERT HALE

© P.J. Gallagher 2020
First published in Great Britain 2020

ISBN 978-0-7198-3087-7

The Crowood Press
The Stable Block
Crowood Lane
Ramsbury
Marlborough
Wiltshire SN8 2HR

www.bhwesterns.com

Robert Hale is an imprint
of The Crowood Press

Typeset by
Derek Doyle & Associates, Shaw Heath
Printed and bound in Great Britain by
4Bind Ltd, Stevenage, SG1 2XT

My children Sean, Siobhan and Roderick

CHAPTER ONE

Josh Martin sat frozen with terror. His left hand gripped the iron rail bounding the edge of the seat, while the other scrabbled frantically along the surface of the leather, seeking to find any imperfection that would allow him to maintain his precarious position. Meanwhile, the stagecoach continued to gently sway back and forth in a peaceful motion, at total variance to the ghastly position in which the sole passenger found himself.

Rigid with fright at the ghastly predicament into which he was thrust, his eyes stared out across the void towards the opposite wall of the valley from where he was perched, and then, reluctantly, looked down at the view beyond his feet at the ground a thousand feet below him.

Everything had happened so fast. The stagecoach had been moving at a slow, steady clip along the mountain trail on a route seldom used, but one that might cut several hours from their journey, according to Billy Barnes the Jehu. And he should know, having ridden all the routes for nigh-on thirty years.

Billy had been chatting affably to Josh, his only passenger on this particular journey, when there had been a distant rumble, followed by an ever increasing roar as the rocky surface to their right had crumbled away and the wall of the mountain had slid down in a massive landslide. Billy could not turn the team and tried to outrun the tons of stone, small trees, bushes and huge boulders that came bounding down on to the narrow ribbon of the trail. It was a useless endeavour. Despite his efforts, the team tried to turn to the left to avoid the onrushing torrent of stone, and in that direction there was only the lip of the trail and then – open space.

A massive rock, nearly as large as the coach, came rolling down, hit another ahead of it and leapt into the air. Momentarily it looked as though it would go clear over the backs of the team, but it was not to be. Like an evil, malicious force, the boulder smashed into the side of the right-hand horse of the lead pair, driving him relentlessly into the side of his partner and sending the pair of them over the edge into space. Their weight dragged the next pair to a similar doom, and inevitably the remaining pair went with them.

Billy, with the reins wrapped around his arms, was ripped from his seat and hurled, with a despairing scream, like a stone from a catapult out into the void. Inexorably the coach was pulled towards the edge – but providentially, the left front wheel ran up against a young mountain ash, which halted its forward progress, snapping the leather traces and leaving the vehicle teetering precariously on the edge of the void.

As more debris from the landslide struck the coach, Josh realized that the rig was inexorably slewing to the right as pressure mounted against the left side rear wheels. It was time to move before he and his conveyance were thrust beyond the point of no return and sent hurtling down into the valley below.

What could he do? Thoughts raced through his fevered mind as he sought to make a plan that could possibly provide salvation, rather than the oblivion that would obviously be his fate if he did nothing. Could he climb back over the roof of the coach and then take his chances among the oncoming landslide, although the latter was definitely slowing? A slight movement on his part caused the delicately balanced vehicle to rock alarmingly, and Josh hurriedly abandoned that plan.

A glance to his left revealed that the left front wheel was still locked against the young mountain ash, which sturdily resisted the attempts of this foreign object to tear it from the deep crevasses into which it had thrust its roots. The trunk of the ash was about three feet away from his left arm, but every movement tilted his seat farther away if he remained where he was.

Bracing his right foot against the curved flooring, and pushing against the leather seat with his right hand, he released the grip of his left hand on the iron seat support and leaned out in an attempt to grasp the trunk of the young tree. Initially his fingertips merely brushed the rough bark, but he made a superhuman effort to achieve his objective. With his leg and shoulder muscles screaming at the unaccustomed strain, he tried once more and was rewarded as the left hand firmly grasped the trunk of the mountain ash.

Turning his body to the left, he brought his right arm across to grip the iron support with his right hand, and then wriggled forwards until his upper body was suspended between the coach and the tree. As he did so, the coach lurched further into space, and Josh launched himself at the tree, clinging to it desperately with both hands, and with both legs wrapped around the trunk – as in the same moment the stagecoach, with a final long growl, tipped and hurtled down to smash into smithereens in the valley far below.

Josh Martin slid down the trunk of the young mountain ash to stand on the ground, shaking and with his legs trembling, still holding desperately to the tree as though he were afraid that if he let go he would follow the stagecoach into oblivion. As his shaking subsided, he staggered across the rock-strewn track to sink exhausted on to a large boulder. For a long time he just sat there, holding his head in both hands as the full realization of his escape from a gruesome death struck home, and as he absorbed the nature of the predicament in which he now found himself.

Josh raised his head and looked around in despair. He was alone, high on a little used mountain trail, with no likelihood of fellow travellers appearing to offer aid. Life was not supposed to end in this way, he thought resentfully. Is this what it all amounts to? A lonely death from starvation, miles from any fellow human being, and very far indeed from his two aged parents scratching out a living on a hard scrabble farm in northern Indiana.

CHAPTER 2

Three years earlier, when he was fourteen years old, his teacher had permitted him to choose a book to read from the school library (a shelf of volumes stacked below the blackboard). The book of life and adventures in the far West had triggered in him an overwhelming desire to emulate the fictional characters he read about, and despite the entreaties of his mother and the sage advice given by his father, Josh had left home and travelled west, picking up odd jobs that paid for food and accommodation and the cost of travel.

He had met Billy Barnes in a small town in New Mexico, and upon learning that Billy was taking a stagecoach west to Casa Grande where there was said to be a successful gold strike, Josh had asked if he could make the journey as an outside passenger. Billy had agreed, and since it was not to be part of a regular route, had waived the coach fee for the pleasure of having someone to talk to during the long journey.

Now Josh bitterly regretted that meeting, and

wished that it were possible to turn the clock back to when he had been safe at home in Indiana. Full of self pity, he wallowed in his misery and sat motionless for some considerable time.

But finally, it seemed as though a tiny voice inserted itself into the depth of his despair, and he heard his father say, 'Josh, there will be times when you'll believe there is no hope for the future. That is the time when you have to prove to yourself that you are indeed a man, and face every obstacle accordingly. Do so, and in time you will win through!'

Josh raised his head and looked around. He was still alone, but it seemed to him that his father was with him, and with renewed hope he started to evaluate his situation.

First of all he considered his physical situation. At the age of seventeen he was already fully grown and had reached the height of just short of six feet. Raised on a farm and used to manual labour, he knew that he was extremely fit, and aware of the muscles rippling beneath his ragged shirt, had already proved, in several fights with his peers back in Indiana, that he could hold his own.

As regards clothing, the situation could have been far worse. He had lost his hat in the landslide, and had felt his shirt rip when he had strained to reach the tree. But his worn jeans were still in one piece, though frayed at the bottom hems and a trifle threadbare at both knees, and his canvas vest remained intact. For footwear, he still had his stout pair of working boots.

However, when it came to equipment for defence or

as a means to obtain food, he was in a far sorrier state. Emptying his pockets could be done in an instant. From the first he produced his only weapon, a folding knife with two blades, one four inches long but the other a mere stub, having been snapped off in the execution of some long forgotten task. In the other was an unused leather bootlace, two silver dollars and a small number of copper coins. His right vest pocket produced a small sack of Bull Durham tobacco and 'the makings', and in the left a small flat tin containing eight friction matches. That was the sum total of Josh's worldly goods. His canteen, and a carpet bag containing a spare shirt, socks and an old muzzle-loading revolver had gone over the cliff in the disaster that had befallen the stagecoach.

Could anything be retrieved from the wreckage of the stagecoach? Well, the only way to find out would be to climb down to where the remains were located! Was that possible?

Josh walked slowly and unwillingly over to the faithful ash tree, and kneeling down, grasped the trunk firmly: suppressing a shudder, he looked down. In fact the wreckage was immediately below him. The coach had fallen into a grove of pine trees, and these appeared to have absorbed some of the weight of the vehicle – so that instead of hitting the ground directly, when it would have burst asunder, the dense limbs of the trees had provided an element of cushioning which had broken the fall, leaving parts of the conveyance looking relatively intact.

Now, he wondered, was there any way he could get

down to the wreckage? Leaning out he looked long and hard at the cliff surface below him, first to the left, and then to the right. Initially it appeared to be a hopeless proposition from his current location, and he was already thinking of moving further along the track – but then, glancing to the right, he noticed that the face was no longer vertical, but rather sloping at between 75 to 80 degrees. Josh reasoned that, as long as he could find hand- and footholds, and kept his body as flush as possible with the rock face, he should be able to descend, since his weight would not be pulling straight down but rather pressing him towards the cliff.

Should he make the attempt? What if he slipped and fell? He could try to climb down, or he could stay where he was, but probably end up facing a lingering death from starvation. Surely it would be better to die trying, than to surrender to the alternative?

The above notions, and many others, chased through Josh's mind as he surveyed the uninviting rock surface he would have to overcome.

Finally he made up his mind: he would try the descent, or die in its undertaking. Josh rose to his feet and walked to the right, to where he intended to make his attempt. There was a small shrub there growing on the edge of the cliff, and sitting down and rolling on to his stomach, he eased his legs over the edge while grasping the bush with his left hand – then slowly he eased his body back until he was spread-eagled against the cliff.

There was a diagonal fissure in the rocky surface,

and Josh took a firm hold there with his right hand; then hugging the cliff face, he lowered himself, while seeking a firm footing for at least one of his booted feet. And so gingerly, his heart pounding with every move, Josh slowly and cautiously made his way down the side of the mountain, until, hours later it seemed, he stood triumphantly on level ground, staring up at the cliff he had overcome.

After resting for a short while, he made his way across the treacherous scree to where the forlorn remains of the stagecoach lay smashed and torn asunder by the fall. Up close there was very little to indicate that the pile of wreckage had once been a vehicle. The body of the coach had torn through the pine trees and had telescoped together when it hit the ground and exploded with the impact.

Parts that ranged from the broken single tree to a relatively intact door were entangled with broken wheels, leather thorough braces, and the corpses of the six horses. Josh had placed his carpet bag containing all his worldly goods in the rear boot – but in the chaos of the wreckage, it was difficult to identify anything resembling either the forward or the rear boot. He rummaged through the debris, but in the realization that he didn't have a snowball's chance in hell of locating either his bag or anything that he could eat or that would aid him in any way.

Lifting a piece of body panel, he peered underneath and was rewarded by a minor find when he located his old hat, intact. Exploring further, he found a canvas bag, which he remembered as being stowed in the forward boot between Billy Barnes and himself. Billy had emphasized the importance of the bag and its contents, and excitedly, Josh pulled open the drawstring and examined the contents within.

He was bitterly disappointed. The bag contained a large wrench useful for tightening the hub nuts retaining the coach wheels, a screwdriver, and an assortment of nuts and screws – no doubt very useful if you had a stagecoach to maintain, but useless in his present circumstances. Nevertheless there was one thing in the bag that he certainly could use: an old Bowie-style knife in a worn leather sheath, which, Josh surmised, was kept with the other tools if repairs had to be made to any of the leather equipment.

The knife had been kept razor sharp, and Josh welcomed the addition to his limited armoury. He explored the area further out from the location of direct impact, and at length was rewarded by the sight of his canteen, undamaged, hanging from the broken branch of a pine tree. Sadly, much higher up in that same tree could be seen the body of Billy Barnes, wedged securely in a fork. There was no way that Josh could even attempt to retrieve the driver's body and give him a Christian burial, and so he left Billy in his final resting place, consoling himself with the thought that this was almost in keeping with native practices.

Josh found a convenient boulder and sat down to consider his next move. Had his perilous descent to the coach site been worth the effort? Well, he was no worse off than before his climb, and he now had his canteen, a worthwhile knife and his hat. What else could he salvage?

There had been a travelling rug that Billy had suggested Josh could use if he got cold. Now the lad
realized that he could indeed use it, and make it into
a poncho – if it could be found. He looked around,
turning over broken pieces of the curved box that had
been the driver's seat and the forward boot, and eventually unearthed the soiled travelling rug. Josh shook
it out and draped it over a rock, seeking for any other
useful plunder. A small roll of stout-looking twine was
added to his pile, but that was the limit of his success.

Josh began to think of food, having not eaten since
he and Billy had started their journey together. A dis-
tinct rumble from his stomach made him realize that
he was hungry, and saliva began to gather in his mouth
as a reminder from his body saying 'Hey, I'm starving!
Feed me!'

He looked around, and suddenly a somewhat gruesome thought struck him. There was food here if only
he could bring himself to eat it. The horses had only
been dead a few hours, so the meat was still relatively
fresh in that short time. The brown mare, which had
been the right rear horse of the team, lay nearest to
hand; Josh recalled the many times he had assisted in
the slaughter and preparation of pigs for the larder,
and organized himself to perform similar tasks on this
victim of the landslide.

First of all he cleared the undergrowth and dead
brush in a clearing, and built a fire within a circle of
stones: he used dry leaves and small sticks as its base,
and gradually increased the size of the material until

he had a pile of glowing embers. When he had his fire drawing nicely, he cut a number of sticks from several aspens bordering the grove – peeling off the bark and sharpening the ends, he stacked them ready beside his fire. Now for the meat.

Whetting the already sharp blade of the old Bowie, he poured a very small quantity of water on the knife in lieu of sterilization and made his first cut. The haunch of the dead mare was uppermost and, drawing the blade firmly across and at right angles, he peeled back the hide exposing the fat and red flesh below. With sure strokes Josh cut out a chunk of horse meat roughly rectangular in shape and weighing five or six pounds.

Slicing the meat into strips, he impaled these on his aspen sticks and set them over the glowing embers of his fire, with some close above the coals and others higher up, which he thought might be smoked and could be used as future rations when travelling.

While the meat sizzled and dripped hot fat into his fire, Josh attempted to clean his hands, bloody after his butchering tasks. The only way to do this was to sac-rifice a minute amount of his precious water – but he just had to rid himself of the stickiness of the drying blood. At length he was moderately successful, and so he then sat cross-legged and paid more attention to his culinary efforts.

The meat nearest the fire looked charred, and experimentally, he cut off a piece and popped it into his mouth. The morsel was delicious, and Josh rapidly ate the remainder of that strip; he moved another

19

closer to the embers, and consumed that one, too. The meat further away he noted was more dried than truly smoked, since he didn't have a proper smoke house, but he figured it would suffice. Then after a swig of his precious water, Josh banked up his fire, and draping the old rug about his shoulders, prepared to spend his first night alone in the wilderness.

CHAPTER 3

It wasn't a pleasant night's rest. Once Josh had made up his mind, back on the track, that he was going to survive his ordeal, he had been too busy with the physical effort of climbing down the cliff, exploring the wreckage and preparing his meagre repast, to reflect upon his predicament – but as he attempted to sleep, the enormity of his situation pressed down upon him.

Apart from the fact that he was in western New Mexico, or possibly Arizona, Josh had in truth no idea where he was. Billy had been taking the stagecoach to a place named Casa Grande, but his passenger had been content to sit up on the box and listen to the driver's ramblings instead of learning more about the route and the place they were headed to. Presumably, if Josh could climb back up to the track he could attempt to continue on to this town with the reputed gold strike. Alternatively, he could possibly backtrack and attempt to reach the town from which they had started.

Then another thought entered his mind: suddenly

it occurred to him that, whatever his specific location, this was Indian territory. To be more exact, it was country inhabited by Apache Indians, and they had been at war with the white interlopers for many years. Attempts to raise this issue with Billy Barnes when first they had first met had been dismissed by the stage-coach driver as so much talk, and that the actual situation was really quite different.

The thought of Indians coming upon him during the night drove all ideas of sleep from Josh's mind, and he lay there until, in the early dawn, he arose stiff and cold in the harsh mountain air, determined to move from this site as soon as possible. Using the old Bowie knife, he cut down an ash sapling and, swiftly lopping off the small branches, trimmed a five-foot length into a serviceable staff, to be used as an aid to walking; also, mindful of the way he and other boys used to fight with staves, it could, if necessary, be employed as a primitive weapon.

The rug he rolled lengthways with his pieces of par-tially dried horse meat placed in the centre; then he tied it securely at both ends with twine, and then together, thereby creating a horse-collar bundle similar to those used by troops of both sides in the recent civil war. With his 'horse collar' draped over his right shoulder to hang on his left side, and with his water bottle hanging on his right hip, Josh picked up his staff. Kicking dirt over the remains of his fire and with a last look around, he turned his back on the stagecoach carnage and set off resolutely to try and find his way to Mesa Grande.

Keeping the cliff face on his right side, Josh plodded on, picking his way amid areas of scree, fallen boulders and dead undergrowth, which, together with living trees and bushes, did their best to impede his progress. It was hard work, and in a couple of hours he was bathed in perspiration, his shirt sticking to his back like an uncomfortable second skin. Grimly Josh struggled on as the sun rose higher and shone down relentlessly – more and more frequently he had to pause to wipe off the salty sweat streaming down his forehead and stinging his eyes.

Finally, estimating that it was midday, Josh sank exhausted at the base of a large pine tree; partially unrolling his 'horse collar', he extracted a couple of sticks of meat and, with cautious sips from his water bottle, proceeded to break his fast with the now unappetizing semi-dried flesh. How far had he come? Josh thought that maybe, just maybe, he had put a mile, or possibly a little more, between himself and the wreckage. He looked back along the cliff hoping to be able to spot the little mountain ash that had offered him salvation, but it was lost to sight amidst the other foliage that successfully limited his vision.

Turning his gaze away from the cliff, Josh looked down over the valley along which he was toiling.

Miles away, appearing as a misty blue-grey wall, was the other side of the valley, while in between were patches of greenery interspersed with yellowish areas, which denoted sandy soil. Several stony areas suggested dry watercourses, as did the gravel-fringed line running down the centre of the valley, but nowhere

23

was there a sign of surface water.

As he swept his eyes back and forth across the wide valley, Josh's attention was arrested by a wisp of grey smoke curling up into the atmosphere. It disappeared from view, and then, moments later, reappeared. There was next to no wind, and it ascended vertically, becoming larger as the source, a fire of some sort, gained strength.

Josh stood by the pine tree leaning on his staff, undecided as to his course of action. Fire meant human beings – but were they natives or settlers? This far away there was no way of determining whether the smoke indicated potentially hostile or friendly people. In the short time he had been alone since the landslide, Josh had yearned for the sound of a human voice, but now, aware of his locality, he wasn't sure what would be the wisest course of action to choose.

Eventually the notion of potential company won the day, and trying to strike a course that would bring him close to the source of the smoke, Josh set off across the valley. The further he got away from the cliff, the easier was his progress, as the trees spread out, and his way was not impeded by rock falls and scree. As much as possible he kept within the tree line, although this meant his progress followed a zigzag route rather than a straight line, which would have taken him across several wide open areas.

At length he found himself drawing closer to the fire, and he soon realized that the blaze ahead was no simple cooking fire, but a much larger conflagration. Could it be some settler burning off undergrowth, prior to preparing his ground for cultivation? It was possible, but Josh took no chances and ensured that a screen of brush remained in front of him as he covered the last few yards between him and his objective.

At last he halted, and cautiously parting the few branches that obscured his view to the front, peered out. He was horrified by what was disclosed before him.

In a fair-sized clearing a roughly constructed shanty was burning fiercely, the crackling flames licking hungrily at the last unburned boards. Off to one side was a tree, and hanging from a stout branch was the body of a man. He was suspended upside down over a small fire, which had already consumed his hair, and blackened his pain-contorted features. It was obvious that, prior to his final torture, the poor soul had been stripped naked and mutilated by being emasculated and his member cut off. Mercifully, it seemed to Josh that the victim was dead. The same was true of the woman, probably his wife, who, naked, had undoubtedly been raped repeatedly before having her throat cut, as she lay helpless on the ground before their primitive dwelling.

Josh withdrew from the ghastly scene before him. There was absolutely nothing he could do, and realizing that to remain at the spot put his own future in extreme jeopardy, he put as much distance as possible between himself and the savage slaughter. He knew that he could at least have attempted to bury the sorry remains of the murdered couple, but he salved his conscience with the thought that they were already dead, and his first priority was to consider the living, namely one Josh Martin.

CHAPTER 4

As he hurried away he thought, too, about the Indians who could have perpetrated such butchery. Josh did not know very much about the Indians of the South West United States. In fact he did not know much about Indians of any state. But he did know a little about the Apache and their ongoing war against the white settlers, and he had heard the word Mescaleros bandied about, and so he ascribed the work behind him to the aforementioned tribe.

Josh looked down and was horrified to realize that he was leaving a trail of footprints in the sandy soil which anyone, let alone an Apache brave bent on mayhem, could follow with ease. Returning to where he had first observed the results of the Indian raid, he used a dead branch to brush away his footprints, or at least make them appear part of earlier activity around the site. And so he retreated, diligently brushing away evidence of his recent presence and deliberately trying to find stony outcrops where his passing left little or no trace.

Then as he was passing close to one of the rocky outcrops with which the valley abounded, he heard a sound that prompted him to freeze motionless. Straining to hear, he stood poised for flight should the noise denote the presence of an enemy. There! Josh heard the sound again, and then again at regular intervals. Initially he thought that it appeared to be a small animal in pain. Then it sounded as though someone was crying. Moving as silently as was possible, he moved in among the boulders, attempting to determine the source of the sound.

There was a place where a huge mass of rock had fallen in eons past to land squarely across two other pieces, forming a low cavity that extended back several feet, to where more pieces of granite effectively plugged the rear exit. Since the roof at the entrance to this strange cave was but four feet above the ground, Josh had to crouch down to enter, as he sought the origin of the noises that he had heard earlier.

As his eyes grew accustomed to the half-light of the interior, he became aware of a creature crouched down as far from the entrance as it could get – and from it came the sounds that had attracted his attention. Cautiously he moved closer, and tentatively reached out a hand in an attempt to soothe the grief-stricken creature.

Straightaway his fingers encountered not skin or fur, but cloth, and Josh immediately realized that his earlier supposition of a small animal in pain had been sadly in error. The roughly woven substance beneath his right hand was covering a slim human body that froze into quivering silence at his first touch.

'It's all right, lad. Nobody's going to hurt you. You just settle down now!' and he stroked his hand up and down the small back to emphasize his remark. Hearing a human voice speaking English, the person half turned towards Josh, who, as he continued his brotherly ministrations, suddenly found that his fingers were rubbing contoured flesh where hitherto the surface had been smooth. Realization came upon Josh in a flash, and he pulled his hand back, his face burning with embarrassment.

'I'm sorry, Miss. I didn't know. I mean, I didn't intend to be familiar. I just...' and Josh lapsed into silence as the girl in front of him sat up and, crossing her legs, faced him with her head bowed down, sobbing silently to herself.

Josh wriggled around until he was alongside her, and putting his right arm over her shoulder, pulled her to him and sat there while the unknown girl wept.

He didn't know what to do to alleviate her distress. Josh didn't have siblings of either sex, and had had very little to do with any females apart from his mother and her sister Aunt Fanny, who visited at irregular intervals. He had always been taught to respect women as being the weaker sex, and knowing his own physical strength, he had no difficulty accepting the foregoing literally. On the other hand, as he developed and his voiced deepened and his facial hair grew, whenever Aunt Fanny visited she always took pains to warn him of bad women, saying: 'You watch out, young Josh! All women are rotters!' – except, of course, herself and her sister, Josh's mother.

He had failed to grasp the implications of her warning, and to date, he did not think that he had ever stood in danger. True, there had been the time at school when Betsy Mae had wanted him to go behind the stable with the promise that she would show him something new, but Alfie Bateson had made a new slingshot and Josh was anxious to see it in action. So he hadn't gone with Betsy Mae.

Now, he wondered, was the girl next to him a decent person, like his mother, or was she a rotter?

After what to Josh seemed an eternity, the unknown girl raised her head and said listlessly, in a small sad voice, 'My name is Ellie,' followed by the query: 'Who are you?'

In a few whispered sentences Josh told Ellie his name and described his disaster and how he happened to find her, skipping quickly over the horrors of the butchery at the burning cabin. Despite his attempt to avoid that part of his story, somehow the mere reference to the episode was enough to start Ellie shuddering and crying soundlessly as she turned and buried her face in his shoulder, clinging desperately to his shirt with both hands.

Again Josh comforted her in the only way he knew how, which was to hold her tight and pat and stroke her thin little shoulder. After all, that had been the way his mother had always soothed his feelings when, as a small boy, he had turned to her for solace after some unpleasant experience. So he figured that he was doing the right thing.

In a short while Ellie's crying ceased, and wriggling free from Josh's grasp, she demanded unexpectedly, 'Do you have anything to eat? I'm starving!'

Josh, startled by this abrupt change from bereaved, helpless little girl to one declaring a need for nourishment – and obviously expecting that he provide something at a moment's notice – stammered helplessly, and then opened his 'horse collar'. He extracted two of the twigs of dried meat, one of which he offered to Ellie saying, 'Here, chew on this! It don't look like much, but it's all I've got so it'll have to do!'

Ellie took the proffered horse meat, and wrinkling her little nose in disgust, tentatively bit off a small piece and chewed on it, exclaiming 'Ugh! It's awful!' But Josh noticed that she swallowed the morsel and continued eating until she had consumed the whole piece, and then looked expectantly to him to furnish more.

Josh shook his head. 'I'm sorry Ellie, but that is all I can spare at the moment. We will have to hunt if we are going to survive in this awful valley.' And the boy turned and crawled out of the cave, followed reluctantly by Ellie, who was unwilling to leave her place of refuge.

Standing amid the boulders they turned and looked at each other. Ellie saw in Josh a tall, broad-shouldered young man with a mop of unruly brown hair crowning an unshaven face, which, when he smiled, revealed strong white teeth below a pair of penetrating grey eyes. His dress was that common to all of the western states: a blue torn shirt, partially covered by a worn canvas vest, clothed his upper body, and below he wore a pair of ragged jeans. Worn but serviceable boots completed Josh's ensemble.

Josh looked with interest at his recently acquired companion. Ellie barely came up to his shoulder, and he figured that she was approximately five feet, or possibly a little more, in height. She was slim, in fact some might have called her skinny, and was wearing a faded print dress that was obviously made for a person of younger age, since the hem barely reached below her brown knees. For footwear, Ellie was making do with a pair of worn out Mexican sandals, which should have been discarded months ago.

He looked at the girl and grinned. 'Well, Ellie. You and me are a fine-looking pair. I don't think either of us would fetch more than a dollar in any store!' He smiled encouragingly, to show that his remark was not a slight on her appearance, and in return, Ellie offered a sad little sigh of agreement.

In truth, he noted that Ellie was in dire need of some personal grooming. Her straw-coloured hair was unkempt and tangled and would benefit from a good prolonged brushing. Her attractive little face was dirty with tear stains that had run down from her reddened eyes and across her lightly sun-tanned cheeks, and she would undoubtedly improve with a strip-down wash all over.

Immediately Josh went hot with embarrassment at the notion of Ellie standing naked before him, and he hurriedly forced the idea from his mind and bent to fiddle with his bootlace to cover his confusion.

It was providential that he did so, because at the very moment that he crouched, an arrow whirred past him to clatter harmlessly against the rocks. Ellie squealed and scuttled back into her hiding place as Josh turned to face an Apache brave who was almost upon him.

CHAPTER 5

Gray Hawk had not had a very good day. He had woken late with a throbbing head that kept pounding, proof that the mescal he had consumed the night before was, as his squaw Good Woman had insisted, more than ready for consumption.

He had slept on into the late morning while the men of the band had dealt with the pair of White Eyes who had defied the Apache order to depart from the valley. By the time Gray Hawk arrived at the scene, the men had already left, and the fired cabin was just a pile of charred embers. All that was there was the dead woman and her man still swinging from the lone pine tree.

Disgruntled, and with his head still aching, he had cast around seeking he knew not what, and had found the trail that some clumsy White Eye had left. Gray Hawk had followed the faint tracks with ease. Why, an Apache papoose could have done the same, he thought, as he entered the jumble of rocks and saw the two young White Eyes emerge from their hiding place.

Fumbling with excitement Gray Hawk unslung his bow, and reaching behind to the quiver that Good Woman had recently made, extracted an arrow and prepared to send it on its way. The range was short, and the target loomed large before him as he carefully drew back his bowstring and released the arrow.

He was astounded when, despite the White Eyes having his attention not on Gray Hawk but on the female before him, he ducked down to avoid the oncoming arrow. Not bothering to reach for another arrow, Gray Hawk gave a short war cry, and dropping the bow, sprang forwards, drawing his scalping knife as he did so.

Josh reacted to the oncoming Apache by swinging his staff before him in an on-guard position as he advanced to meet his adversary. Gray Hawk placed his knife between his teeth, leaving both hands free to grab the staff of the young White Eyes – and as he did so, he pulled hard. Josh momentarily resisted the pull on the part of Gray Hawk, and then reversed direction, going hand over hand along his staff to get closer. Then, being well balanced, he delivered a mighty kick with his right foot with brutal force right in Gray Hawk's crotch.

The Apache had never been kicked by a solid leather-capped American working boot before – especially in a part of his body that he considered private. A wave of excruciating pain surged up from that area and the knife dropped from his mouth as, howling, he released his grip on the staff and clutched with both hands to protect the injured part. Josh, seeing his enemy so occupied, slipped his grasp on the staff to the very end and whirled it around his head, then brought it against the side of the other's head with an almighty thwack that knocked him unconscious.

Josh realized that he had to work quickly, and called upon Ellie to help him: 'Ellie come here! Quickly now, we must hurry!'

Ellie peered out of the cave fearfully, but made no move to come any further. 'Is he dead, Josh? Did you kill him?'

'No, you little dolt. He's not dead, but we will be if you don't come and help me tie him up!'

While Josh was trying to answer Ellie's questions, he was also rolling the Apache on to his stomach and trying to bring the unconscious man's hands together behind his back. Ellie reluctantly knelt down beside him, but made no attempt to assist.

Josh, exasperated by her unhelpfulness, roared at the girl: 'Ellie! Grab hold of his hands from me and hold them while I tie his thumbs together!'

Her reaction was to bite her bottom lip and shake her head. 'Ugh! I couldn't do that, Josh!' and then in a matter-of-fact little voice suggested: 'Why don't you just kill him?'

'Cos I'm not a savage, that's why! Now do as I tell you!' Slowly the girl did as she was told, and Josh employed short pieces of twine to expertly tie Gray Hawk's thumbs together; he gave each finger the same treatment. By the time Josh had completed the operation, the Apache was slowly becoming aware of his situation, and sensed that he was not at home in his wickiup. By the time he was fully conscious Josh had rolled him over and tied his ankles in such a way that would permit him to walk, but to take only short steps.

The young White Eyes stepped back to admire his handiwork, and it was as well that he did so, as Gray Hawk, now fully awake, raised his loosely bound feet and directed a lethally intended kick at Josh's shins; however, he was brought up short by the rope tying his feet.

Captor and prisoner stared at each other in silence. Gray Hawk was filled with hate for the young man before him, coupled with a mixture of shame that he should be bested by one who was merely a youth rather than a seasoned warrior. As he glared up he could not help wondering about his eventual fate. Was he to be kept as a slave, perhaps? Or would he be sacrificed to some strange White god? Or, worse of all, was he to be used as food by the two young White Eyes? There was no way of knowing what terrible thoughts filled their minds.

Josh looked down, filled with boyish triumph at the thought that he had won a combat with one of the dreaded Apache – but he was equally concerned with the problem of what to do with his prisoner. Ellie's advice came to the forefront of his mind, and was swiftly dismissed. No, he just couldn't kill an unconscious human being, nor, for that matter, one that was bound and totally helpless before him. True, he reasoned, in the heat of battle I would certainly kill, but that is a different situation. Josh wished that he could communicate with his captive, then perhaps they could reach an understanding – but then he figured that was impossible under the present circumstances.

Ellie's thoughts were far more basic. She was filled with loathing as she stared down at the Apache, and considered that he could quite possibly have been one of the savages who had raped and then killed her mother. She just could not understand why Josh had not exterminated this one. If you encounter an unpleasant insect on the ground, you stamp on it to get rid of it. So what was the difference?

Josh and Ellie stood in silence, each contemplating the dilemma before them, until querulously the latter proclaimed: 'Well, Josh, are we going to stand all day staring at this wretched savage, or are we going to make plans to get away from this awful place? Equally, what are we going to do about food and water? I'm still hungry!'

Josh rounded on her. 'Ellie, all you seem to think about is your belly!' Then, aware that he had made a quite humourous rhyming remark, he started giggling, and the girl, catching the drift of 'Ellie/belly', joined in the laughter, while Gray Hawk glared up at them, convinced they were deciding his fate.

Finally Josh shrugged his shoulders, and opening up his 'horse collar', produced the last three sticks of the dried horsemeat. He handed one to Ellie, and then, after a moment's hesitation, offered one to Gray Hawk, while he chewed on the third.

Gray Hawk was hungry. He had left the camp angrily attempting to catch up with the war party, and with his head still full of mescal, had not bothered to

38

break his fast. Now saliva gathered in his mouth as he watched the two White Eyes chewing on the meat, and tentatively he bit on the stick that was presented to him.

Though Ellie kept her thoughts to herself, she was disgusted, shocked that Josh would give their last piece of food to a savage – and not just any old savage, but one who had probably taken part in the killing of her family. So all three of the strange trio chewed away on the dried horsemeat, each with his own thoughts about the repast.

Josh produced his water bottle and shook it. There was only a small amount remaining, and he indicated that they could have but a sip. Ellie took the first and reluctantly handed back the water bottle. Josh quickly put the canteen to his mouth and allowed the faintest of water trickles to emerge and moisten his throat. Pulling a wry face he shrugged his shoulders and put the spout of the canteen to the Apache's lips.

Gray Hawk was thirsty. The natural salt from the blood of the dried horsemeat, coupled with the effect of an earlier bout of drinking mescal, had left him with a raging thirst where his tongue seemed to be three times its normal size and threatened to choke him.

He had watched the young White Eyes with avid interest as they shared what was obviously a small quantity of the life-giving fluid, and was startled when he, too, was offered the last drips from the bottle.

First food and now water! These were strange ways to treat a prisoner, especially when it was obvious that both commodities were in very short supply!

Meanwhile there was a devil inside his throat as his desire for liquid fought against his natural Apache stoicism – and finally won.

'Water!' he muttered in the tongue of The People, and the two White Eyes looked at him curiously. Again he muttered the Apache word for water, but they obviously did not understand. Desperately he sought to find a common term. He did not know the language of these White Eyes – but what of the others who lived far to the south? He knew a few words of their tongue, including the one he desired.

'El agua! El agua!' He struggled to a sitting position, and motioned with his head towards the empty canteen lying beside him while repeatedly muttering the same words in Spanish.

Initially Josh and Ellie sat open mouthed at hearing their captive speak, and they both struggled to make out the meaning of his words. Actually it was Ellie who finally figured out that he was asking for water, and Josh who, seeing the repeated nods of the head and signals with the eyes tied to the same words, determined that possibly he was trying to indicate that he could lead them to water.

Josh got behind Gray Hawk and lifted him to his feet, warily mindful of the latter's kicking power. Then picking up the canteen and holding it up in front of the Apache he said enquiringly, 'Water! El agua?'

Gray Hawk, hampered by his limited gait and ill balanced by his bound hands, shuffled forwards among the rocks, leading them further away from Ellie's refuge. The boy and girl followed, with Josh bringing the Apache weapons in addition to his own equipment, and Ellie fearfully bringing up the rear.

Their pace was funereally slow. The sun beat down remorselessly as the trio staggered along until they reached a point where a gigantic rock loomed overhead, casting the whole area in welcome shadow. Gray Hawk turned to a cleft in the rocky surface and said repeatedly, 'El agua! El agua!'

Josh moved ahead of him and entered the cleft – and there in front of him was a natural basin two or three feet in diameter and perhaps a foot or two deep, filled with limpid clear water shimmering in the gloom. Josh unslung his canteen, and dipping it into the cool liquid, rapidly filled it – then turning back to the others, offered up the spout to the eagerly awaiting Apache while motioning Ellie to enter the cleft and take her fill.

Replete, the strange trio sank down among the rocks savouring the experience of the water surging through the core of their very being, renewing their energy.

Josh was in a quandary. Despite the fact that his Apache captive had appeared increasingly docile when in need of water, he was quite certain that now the Indian had had his fill, to release him from his bonds would be like freeing a savage lion from its cage. Despite this foreboding, Josh's instinct was to trust the man who had led two of his enemies to a place where there was water. The alternative would have been for the three of them to die a lingering death as their bodies dehydrated.

Josh couldn't resolve his problem and, after a lengthy rest, he rose to his feet indicating to the others to rise and continue the journey. But Ellie protested: 'Josh, I can't go on, I'm exhausted!'

'Ellie, if you stay here you'll die! Get up and get moving!' His remarks were delivered in a tone that rejected any notion of discussion, and the girl, after sticking out her tongue and calling him a beast, rose to her feet, reluctant to resume her purgatory.

Gray Hawk obeyed the summons immediately. The liquid he had consumed had washed away the after-taste of the previous evening's drinking bout, and had left him completely refreshed and ready to seize any opportunity to regain his freedom.

They left the boulder-strewn area and made steady progress across a flat, arid wasteland, with the occasional Joshua tree and stunted cacti relieving the monotony. There was no animal life to be seen, and no shade in which to rest as they struggled on with the sun beating down remorselessly. At length Josh called a brief halt, and each was allowed to take a small sip of water from the canteen. Then it was on again, plodding through sandy soil that appeared to delight in hindering their progress.

The plain ended. Josh had been keeping the cliff, down which he had descended, on his right side, so he assumed they were still progressing towards Casa Grande – but suddenly the ground ahead of them fell away, as though a gigantic hand had gouged away the surface, and the trio found themselves on the lip of a precipice with the outline of a long-dead watercourse below them. Mindful of the need to keep close to the cliffs, Josh turned to the right, and he and his companions picked their way along the edge of the crater that loomed before them.

The disaster that next struck was totally unexpected. Josh was in the lead, with Gray Hawk shuffling along behind, his stride restricted by the cord binding one ankle to the other. Ellie was bringing up the rear muttering to herself, no doubt protesting against the endless walking. Suddenly a rattlesnake, sunning itself on a boulder by the dim trail they were following, chose to object violently to their presence. Its head rose, the rattles giving but short warning of its hostile intent, and it struck out at the closest human being. That happened to be Gray Hawk's right leg, which the snake bit. He cried out and instinctively stepped to his left, but was brought up short by the ankle cord. His left foot landed on a loose piece of shale, which rocked and sent him completely off balance. If he had not been bound it is quite possible that he could have recovered his balance – but it was not to be. He teetered on the edge of the precipice and suddenly fell with a despairing cry, bouncing from rock to rock into the depths below to end up with a sickening thud on the stony ground of the dry watercourse.

Ellie shrank back, appalled by the sudden demise of one that she had hated, yet whom she had reluctantly come to accept in the short time that he had been with them. Josh reacted defensively, dropping all of his burdens apart from his staff, which he used to strike the snake repeatedly before it could escape into a hole. His efforts were successful, as the heavy end of his staff struck the reptile on the head, turning it into a lifeless pulp.

Josh stared at the dead rattlesnake, shuddering as he considered how close he had come to experiencing the fate of his Apache captive, and momentarily reflecting that his decision to leave the man bound had probably contributed to his death. Then a more prosaic thought occurred to him: the snake was food! Folks claimed that rattlesnake tasted just like chicken. Well, shortly they were going to find out!

Drawing his Bowie knife he approached the lifeless body, though as a precaution, placed his staff just behind the head and held it there by pressing down with his boot. Then bending down, he rapidly cut off the serpent's head and threw it over the edge of the precipice. Having cut off the rattles, he drew his knife down the body and peeled off the skin revealing the pink flesh.

Ellie approached, drawn by curiosity yet repulsed by the sight of the skinned snake. 'What are you going to do with that, Josh?' she inquired.

'We're going to eat it!' stated her male companion. 'But first I've got to find a place where we can make a little fire. Come on!' And with the skinned snake in his left hand and his trusty staff in his right, he set off along the edge of the cliff looking for a suitable spot where he could attempt to improve his culinary skills. Glumly Ellie followed.

CHAPTER 6

Three hours of steady walking brought them to a place where the edge of the precipice curved round as the valley below ended in a box canyon. At some time in the distant past a huge waterfall must have surged from this location, tearing the ground for centuries and creating the canyon that led into the main valley. The ground was very broken, and finally Josh found a level, secluded spot where he decided to build his cooking fire. 'Ellie! Would you please gather small dry sticks and leaves?'

Ellie, who was feeling pangs of hunger, scurried around as Josh made a circle of stones and proceeded to create a pyramid of sticks with a bed made of a mixture of dry leaves and grass that his companion gathered. Applying one of his precious matches to the pyramid, he soon had a small fire glowing, and by adding more sticks created a bed of red hot embers.

Pouring a trickle of water on to a flat rock, he put the dead snake on its surface and sliced it into pieces about three inches long; these he then stuck on to sharpened sticks and suspended them over his fire at 45 degrees or so, holding the sticks in place with stones.

Ellie appeared with a contribution to the forthcoming meal. 'Josh, look what I've found!' she cried, and proudly showed him her uplifted skirt in which nestled six small brown eggs. 'I think they are grouse or plover eggs. I thought we could cook them somehow and have them with the snake meat!'

Josh, aware that Ellie was trying to prove that she could be just as much a helper, thanked her for her offering and suggested that, after piercing a small hole in each egg, they could place them on a stone close to the embers and let them bake. And the two of them squatted down and tended to the cooking, turning the eggs and meat until they figured that the eggs were baked and the meat charred and ready to eat.

Cracking the shells and picking away the broken pieces they both simultaneously popped a hot egg into their mouth, lamenting at the lack of salt. The six eggs were quickly consumed, and they turned their attention to the meat, tearing it off the bones and attempting with limited success to remove it from between the joints of the snake's backbone.

While thus engaged Ellie gave Josh a brief outline of her story. The two murdered people Josh had seen were not her real parents. They had died four years earlier during an outbreak of some unspecified sickness among the members of the wagon train in which they were going to California. Ellie had been left an orphan, and was left in a community through which the wagons passed.

Ruby, a dance hall performer, had taken pity on the child and taken her in, and over time had become her foster mother. Then Kurt had turned up and started living with Ruby as they wandered from town to town. He wasn't unkind to Ellie, but seemed to tolerate her because of her mother. That is, until recently, when they moved to the shack where they were supposed to be looking for gold. As Ellie developed into a young woman she found that Kurt paid more attention to her, and several times, Ruby had to speak sharply to him. Eventually, Ellie was surprised when her foster mother took her to one side and warned her not to go off alone with Kurt, ever, at any time.

It was shortly after that incident that Kurt approached her one morning while Ruby was fixing a meal for the three of them, and suggested that they go for a little walk. Ellie refused and he had put his arm around her and started fondling her breast. Ellie had broken free and run off, while, back at the shack, male and female voices were raised in anger and only diminished as she put more distance between herself and the quarrelsome pair. She had continued to run, until she found herself among the rocks, and it was then that she heard the war whoops and smoke rising as their primitive home burned. Discovering the cave, she had entered it and crouched there terrified until at length Josh had found her.

Josh listened to Ellie's pitiful story in silence, not sure what to say. He found that he wanted to comfort

47

her, but was afraid to do so physically in case she inter-
preted the gesture as proving that he was no different
from the dead Kurt. If he offered to take care of the
girl, again she might misunderstand him and think he
knew not what. So Josh remained silent and thereby
earned Ellie's displeasure.

Finally he spoke up: 'Well, Ellie, despite all that has
happened we've got to stick together and win this fight
for survival. Now that we've finished eating we must
move quickly from this place and find a more secure
location where we can rest for the night. Come on, up
you get.'

So saying, Josh kicked dirt over the dying embers of
their fire and scattered the rocks encircling the location before gathering his staff, Gray Hawk's bow, and
the quiver with its five remaining arrows; then slipping
his horse collar and canteen around his neck, he prepared to resume their trek.

As they made their way along the edge of the
canyon Josh noticed that the cliffs to his right seemed
lower than before, which, since the mountains could
hardly have sunk, meant that the ground over which
they were walking was rising; the coniferous ground
cover was increasing. Hopefully these were all signs
that they were reaching the end of the valley.

The sun was descending rapidly when Josh called a
halt in a small clearing amid the undergrowth. A rocky
outcrop on one side of the clearing with an apprecia-
ble overhang offered shelter in the event of bad
weather and possible protection from attack in that
direction.

48

He had noticed an increasing number of small animal trails as they left the desert behind, and thought that it might be possible to set out a number of snares and obtain their next meal in that fashion. Therefore, bidding Ellie prepare a fireplace and gather a quantity of dry sticks, he set off to lay various traps, employing cord and a running noose in likely places, and a delicately balanced rock in another hoping that his dead-fall trap might catch some unwary creature.

CHAPTER 7

Josh was gone for quite some time, and Ellie grew increasingly uncomfortable with the silence. It was with great relief that she heard him coming back to the clearing. Her relief, however, rapidly turned to dismay when the bushes parted and two strangers entered the clearing, dragging an unwilling burro.

They both stopped short at the sight of Ellie standing before them in her torn dress and dishevelled in appearance. They stared at her, and leaving the burro, walked forwards and around her, both of them looking at her with hot, lascivious eyes, licking their lips in anticipation. One of them spoke: 'Well, little girlie! What are you doing out here by yourself all alone in the wilderness?'

Ellie, terrified, stammered a reply: 'I'm not alone! My brothers are close by and will be back here immediately.'

One of them slipped an arm around her waist and pulled her close, holding his bearded face inches from hers and breathing a repulsive mixture of stale liquor and tobacco over her, as he sought to kiss her while his other hand tore at the front of her dress.

His companion, not to be outdone, plucked at him and Ellie, crying: 'Lemme have a go Bert! Don't be a hog. Share an' share alike. That's our motto!' and he started to raise Ellie's dress and force his hand between her legs.

Suddenly he stopped and his hand fell away as he toppled forwards with an arrow buried in his back.

Bert, unaware of his companion's demise, continued with his assault on Ellie's person until he received an almighty blow in the middle of the back which sent excruciating pain up and down his spine. He let go of Ellie, turning in anger and agony to where he thought that his partner was standing.

'Whatcha do that for, Tom?' his voice slowing to zero as he realized that Tom was no longer in the land of the living, but was lying dead at his feet. Even as he noted the fact that his pard had been killed with an Apache arrow, there was the twang of a bowstring as yet another arrow came from the bushes and thudded into his stomach, doubling him over with both hands clutching at the shaft. His knees buckled and slowly he collapsed forwards, his knees hitting the ground in a prayerful position before he slumped over as life left him.

Ellie stood there clutching at her torn dress with both hands, petrified by the dead men before her and terrified by the thought that she was now in the hands of the dreaded Apache – when Josh walked into the clearing. He had Gray Hawk's bow in his left hand with an arrow notched and ready to draw as he stared grimly at his two victims. On seeing the pair assaulting Ellie he had not stopped to think but had reacted instinctively, dimly thankful that he had hunted with a homemade bow and arrows as a youth back in Indiana.

Relief flooded through Ellie as the truth of the situation struck her like a blow, and she threw herself forwards and into his arms 'Oh, Josh! I've never been so glad to see you. Those men were terrible, and they wanted to do awful things to me. And you saved me!' and she covered his face with kisses while Josh stood there, his attention still on the dead men, but simultaneously conscious of a warm feeling inside him as his body responded to Ellie's attentions.

Finally, practicalities took over. 'That's enough of that, Ellie. We've got things to do!' He told her how he had been returning to their camp when he saw the men entering the clearing, and that he had done what had to be done. He proceeded to examine the men and their belongings to see what he could find out about the men he had killed.

Both men wore frontier garb and boots, and both were armed with pistols. The one with the arrow in his back had a tip up .32 calibre Smith and Wesson rimfire revolver in a home-made leather holster with cartridges in a belt pouch. His companion had been armed with a heavier weapon, namely a .44 calibre Remington muzzle-loading revolver in a military-style holster, and he had a number of factory-made paper cartridges in a cardboard box together with percussion caps.

Removing both guns and their belts with other accoutrements and putting them to one side, Josh unwillingly searched the men's pockets. Folding knives, chewing tobacco and a number of small denomination coins were his sole reward. Neither man had any kind of identification on him.

He and Ellie next turned their attention to the burro standing patiently by as though awaiting his turn for examination. Untying the canvas-covered packs and removing the pick and shovel lashed alongside, they spread the contents on a folded tarpaulin.

The first thing they noted was that the objects bore no relation to either of the two dead men. There was a suit of store-bought clothing, made for a much shorter man than either of the corpses. There was also a dress carefully wrapped up in paper. The dress, when Ellie held it up against her own body, was found to be about her size, and she quietly decided that later she would exchange it for her own ragged attire.

Cooking utensils in the form of a frying pan, a coffee pot and an enamel mug and dinner plate, together with a single knife, fork and spoon set, suggested the equipment of a man travelling alone, and that he had ample supplies for his own use. There was a sack of flour, coffee beans, a slab of bacon, several cans of beans and even one of peaches.

The contents of the packs and the tools pointed to the previous owner having been a prospector, which seemed at total variance to the two dead men. Josh and Ellie looked at each other, both thinking the same thing, but both hesitating to state what was in their minds.

Josh broke the silence: 'Ellie, it would seem that we have been given the means with which to escape from this valley. I didn't mean to kill those men, but to me, it appears that they didn't come by all this stuff lawfully. They have stolen it, and in my mind that means that, since they're dead, we can use it to help save ourselves.'

Ellie was quick to agree. Already in her mind she was wearing the dress from the pack and cooking a mess of bacon and beans, with the result that her mouth was full of saliva in anticipation of the forthcoming meal. But first they had to get rid of the two corpses. Josh tied a rope around the feet of one man, and using the burro, dragged the body to the edge of a deep gully; then untying the line, he toppled it over into the depths below. He returned to the clearing and repeated the same burial procedure with the other man. He didn't know any suitable prayers, and under the circumstances, didn't think it mattered. They had obviously lived violently and had died violently, and that was that!

While Josh disposed of the bodies, Ellie started fixing the intended meal by starting a fire the way Josh had done, making sure that the wood used was dry and that the little smoke created was lost against the rock of the overhang. She poured some of their precious water into the coffee pot and set the utensil to boil on the fire; then she sliced some of the bacon, and placing it in the frying pan, set it sizzling on the glowing coals. Then using Josh's Bowie knife, with difficulty she opened a can of beans and added them to the bacon.

Not having a coffee grinder, all she could do with the beans was to pound several in a twist of her old dress between two rocks and then pour the crumbled results into her boiling water. Josh, having completed the unpleasant task of getting rid of the two bodies, came and squatted down by the fire, and watched her culinary efforts with great interest.

He thought for a moment and then, mixing some of the flour with a little water, he created a primitive dough, which he rolled and then twisted around a peeled stick. He then suspended the result over the fire, where it browned into a crust.

At length both could wait no longer. Setting the pan upon a large flat rock, they proceeded to eat the bacon and beans, taking turns to use the only spoon. It was the same with the coffee simmering on the coals: they had just the one mug, and therefore sipped in turn at the hot liquid. While eating, Josh had continued to periodically twist the dough-covered stick around until he was satisfied that all was brown, at which point he broke off a piece and handed it to his companion.

'Here Ellie, dip this in the pan!' So saying, he too took a piece of the twisted dough, and dipping it into the frying pan, conveyed the crunchy result to his mouth, and chewed it with great satisfaction. Ellie lost no time in following suit, and between them they rapidly demolished the contents of both frying pan and coffee pot, in addition to the baked dough from the peeled stick.

The meal completed, Ellie and Josh looked at each

other and grinned, both declaring that the late repast was the best they had ever had, thus confirming the well known adage that the circumstances govern the degree to which a meal is appreciated.

'What now, Josh?' queried Ellie, reluctant to make a move after the enjoyment of the food, and the satisfaction that she had taken the main part in preparing it.

Josh, ever practical, declared that he would clean up, which he proceeded to do by scouring the frying pan with sand in lieu of water, and indicating to Ellie that maybe she could find a private place where she could at last remove her dirty torn apparel and put on the dress from the burro's pack. Ellie, nothing loath, grabbed the offered dress and vanished into the bushes, reappearing almost immediately in her new attire.

'Well, that didn't take long!' Josh smiled at his companion. 'Here! Add this to your new appearance!' and he handed her the holster containing the Smith & Wesson revolver.

Ellie shook her head in bewilderment. 'But Josh, I don't know anything about guns! What do I do with it?'

Josh, who had never handled such a pistol but was familiar with firearms in a general way, and had used a rifle for hunting back in Indiana, took the holster back from her; extracting the gun, he quickly gave her a general explanation of the model and how it functioned. He first pressed a little stud forward of the cylinder, and showed how this catch allowed the barrel to be hinged up, permitting the cylinder to be removed. He then showed her how, by inserting the short rod beneath the barrel into the front of each chamber, the little .32 caliber cartridges, or empty cases, could be extracted.

Reloading the revolver, he had Ellie do the same operation until she was familiar with loading and unloading, and then, with an empty cylinder, showed her how to use a two-handed grip to hold, cock and fire the pistol.

'Later, Ellie, I'll let you fire a couple of rounds from your gun, but now I don't want to risk attracting any Apache who may be around. So just load it, and we'll adjust that belt and holster so that you're comfortable with the rig.' So saying, he helped her to find a waist position so that the holster was comfortable on her left hip and she could cross-draw with ease.

Having organized Ellie, Josh turned his attention to the .44 Remington with which he was familiar, although he had never owned one, having had to be content with the shaky old Navy Colt that he had lost when the stagecoach went over the cliff. The Remington had been well cared for and was already loaded and capped, although, as was common with most sensible pistol owners, the hammer rested on an empty chamber.

Darkness was falling on the land by the time that they had completed their examination of the weapons and the material they had acquired, and so they prepared to spend yet another night in the wilderness. There was a difference, however. Ellie now curled up close to Josh, using the tarpaulin as a ground sheet and sharing a tattered blanket and his home-made poncho for cover as the air got progressively cooler

Josh did not object to her presence. In fact, he found himself enjoying the closeness of her thin little body, and turning over, he threw a protective arm across her, which prompted Ellie to snuggle even closer. And thus passed yet another night.

CHAPTER 8

Meanwhile, several miles away and far below, Little Buffalo was having an unsuccessful day hunting, despite having gone farther afield in an area that was new to him. As he started thinking about a dry camp, while chewing on a strip of dried meat, he saw what looked like the body of an animal lying amid the rocks of a small arroyo. He approached, and saw to his dismay that it was the bound body of his friend Gray Eagle. Little Buffalo stood over the battered corpse and, looking up, tried to re-enact the tragedy. From the way his friend had been tied, it was obvious to him that Gray Eagle had been deliberately killed by being cast down from the plateau far above, either as some form of sacrifice or merely because he was one of The People.

It was now too dark to try and ascend the cliff and seek more information about the death of his friend, so, quietly singing a death song, he sat by the body of Gray Hawk and awaited the dawn.

*

In the morning the white travellers arose and Ellie organized some hot coffee and 'twist' bread while Josh inspected his traps. There was but one victim – an unwary black-tailed jackrabbit had been snared in the night and was a welcome addition to their larder. Josh gutted it, then returned to camp, pleased that he had been successful.

After a quick breakfast of bread and coffee, they made packs of their belongings and lashed them on to the burro, which was placidly munching away at any low-hanging foliage it was able to reach. Josh debated skinning and cooking the jackrabbit before travelling, and later wished that he had, because in the hot sunshine, the meat rapidly became high, and eventually he had to dump it in a ravine.

Far behind them Little Buffalo had finally reached the top of the cliffs, although he had had to backtrack a considerable distance in order to find a location suitable for climbing. Now successful, he stood on the edge and looked down to where the body of his friend lay. Casting around, he gradually developed a picture of what must have happened. He imagined his friend, bound and helpless, being pushed towards the edge of the cliff, while as part of some strange, evil ceremony, a rattlesnake was simultaneously killed and skinned.

Cautiously the Apache brave followed the trail, and soon found a place where there had been a fight, resulting in the demise of two of the White Eyes. So Gray Hawk had succeeded in killing two of the evil ones before they had overpowered him. Little Buffalo thought that Gray Hawk's death must have been shortly after his coup, since he hadn't had time to retrieve his arrows from the bodies, which had been unceremoniously dumped in a deep cleft. Little Buffalo shook his head in disgust. So the White Eyes didn't even treat their own dead with dignity! He decided that, rather than following the trail, it was time to return to the village and inform the elders of what had happened, and see what kind of action the council decided was needed.

CHAPTER 9

Apart from the loss of the rabbit meat, they had an uneventful day as they struggled on; they still kept the cliffs on their right side, but these were much lower now, as they neared the end of the valley. Shortly after midday, noticing a patch of thick undergrowth, they cautiously entered it and found a small trickle of water that bubbled up from an underground spring before it sank rapidly back into the sandy soil. Josh used the shovel they had acquired to dig a hole, which quickly filled with water; after it had slowly cleared, they filled both canteens and gave themselves and their faithful burro plentiful drinks before continuing with their journey.

By the third day Josh and Ellie had established a routine so that, working together, they completed the necessary tasks in far less time, which meant they could hit the trail earlier. But that morning they had a rude interruption to their journey: it happened after they had been walking for about an hour, and were passing through an area of jumbled rocks that were strewn around as though some gigantic child had left his playground in a mess. Josh, leading the burro, had just rounded a rock as big as a house and was out of Ellie's sight as she brought up the rear, when he felt a hard object rammed in the middle of his back, and a voice snarled: 'Just keep those hands high, mister, or I'm gonna separate your backbone with a load of buck-shot!'

Josh's hands shot heavenwards as he speedily obeyed the summons, saying: 'Take it easy with that scattergun, whoever you are. If you're out to rob us I'm afraid you're sure out of luck!'

The voice behind the twin muzzles painfully pressing against his spine chuckled sarcastically. 'Me rob you is it? An' you leading my Jacob as bold as brass, as though that burro belonged to you!'

His voice suddenly trailed off as he in turn felt a hard object pressing into the back of his neck, and a female voice cried out; 'You'd better lower that gun away from Josh or I'm going to put a bullet right in the back of your head! Quickly now! I haven't got all day!'

Startled, the owner of the shotgun removed the weapon from Josh, and holding it by the muzzle, held both of his arms out to the side, away from his body. 'Don't you do anything hasty, Miss, with that there gun, please!' – and knowing full well that many females were excitable and prone to do things on impulse, he remained rigid with both arms out-stretched as though crucified, while Josh turned round and gently removed the shotgun from his grasp.

The short, elderly stranger sought to stress to both

Josh and Ellie that he was not a danger to them. He was small, no taller than Ellie, with a round, open face partly covered by several days' growth of whiskers. He was very anxious that they accept his story.

'You've got to believe me! I meant no harm. That there scattergun ain't even loaded. Them scum what took ole Jacob,' nodding with his head at the burro, 'took my powder and caps with them when they left, laughing at the trick they'd played on me. Left me tied up with naught but an empty gun. But they didn't reckon on ol' Ben Johnson getting free and getting on their trail!'

He stopped speaking and looked suspiciously at Josh: 'But how come old Jacob is coming along with you? Are you friends of them varmints that jumped me, or did you buy him from them?'

Josh shook his head, smiling at the thought of being associated with the two robbers, and he motioned for Ben Johnson to lower his arms and for Ellie to holster her pistol. Then, indicating that they should all sit and be comfortable, he gave the old-timer a brief but detailed account of their adventures from when the stagecoach went over the cliff, describing how he had saved Ellie and rid the world of the two scoundrels.

Ben sat there open-mouthed, and when Josh finally ended his narrative, he burst out laughing, slapping his knee and declaring that he couldn't have done better himself. Then, becoming serious, he explained that he had been headed for Casa Grande, having learned of the gold strike there, and he wondered if the three of them should maybe join forces – at least until they reached the diggings, since they were apparently headed in the same direction.

Josh looked at Ellie and raised an eyebrow with a questioning look. She shrugged her shoulders as if to indicate that she didn't object to Ben's company, therefore Josh agreed with the older man's proposal. He would share the limited supplies that were rightfully his. Josh would try to supplement the food supplies by hunting, and Ellie would employ her culinary skills and keep the three of them fed.

Ben did not object to Ellie wearing the dress intended for a favourite granddaughter back east. He had bought it with the firm intention of going back to a place in Illinois where he had family, but then the gold fever had hit him when he heard of the strike at Casa Grande, and so the garment had remained in his pack.

Both Josh and Ben estimated that they should be able to reach their objective in three or four days, barring any unforeseen situation, and so the strange trio proceeded on their journey, continually aware of the need to watch out for any sign of hostile Apaches.

The terrain over which they were travelling continued to show evidence of huge cataclysmic events, events that had taken place eons before the coming of any man, either red or white, to the area. Huge rocks littered the ground, creating a maze through which they made their way, while individual spires detached from the red face of the cliffs to their right suggested that the hand of some mighty sculptor had been at work. Apart from a solitary eagle hovering almost motionless thousands of feet above, there was no sign of life, and the only sound was that of Jacob's little hoofs as he picked his way across the stone-covered surface.

Eventually the trio found that they were going down into a lower valley with high cliffs on either side, red stained from the iron ore in the stone. Far off could be seen a gigantic gash in the side of the cliffs to their right, as though somebody had scooped out a huge hollow. Though remarkably clear in the mountain air and appearing close, it would be at least two full days' march before they were close to that location.

Desert vegetation became more plentiful. Yucca plants, Spanish bayonet, varieties of cacti and the occasional Joshua tree, and in several places patches of tough wiry grass, fought to survive in this hostile environment. They came to a spot that offered the possibility of water between two rocks where the sandy soil appeared damp, and it was decided to camp there. Josh went off to try his luck with snares. Ellie got a small smokeless fire going, and Ben took his shovel and dug a hole in the damp area in the hope of finding water.

The small meal that Ellie put together was again bacon and beans supplemented by 'twist bread', the making of which she was becoming quite an expert at. The empty bean can was not thrown away, but rather had a secondary use as an improvised coffee mug.

During the meal Ellie made a serious announcement: 'Either we're going to have to find other meat, or we're going to have to find a store, because I can't stretch the supplies to last more than two more days. Maybe I can weaken the coffee, or use the grounds twice over, but that's all!'

Ellie's observations were not very comforting to her companions, but there was nothing to be done, and they could only hope that the next day would bring a change in the food situation.

The next morning Josh set out to examine his snares, while Ellie listlessly blew on the coals to encourage a small flame and thereby save using a match to start the fire. Meanwhile, Ben searched the surrounding area in the hope of finding an edible plant or a reptile suitable for the pot.

'Success!' The reappearance of Josh waving a large jackrabbit by the hind legs spurred the campsite into a hive of activity. Seemingly in no time, Ellie had reduced her fire to a large number of glowing hot coals. Josh had skinned, gutted and cleaned his catch, and Ben had constructed a primitive spit using two forked sticks and the steel ramrod from his muzzle-loading shotgun. Master rabbit was impaled on the rod and suspended over the coals, being turned occasionally to ensure that all parts of him received the full benefit of the heat below.

The three waited impatiently for the rabbit flesh to be cooked enough to be devoured, grinning at each other and experiencing the saliva gathering in their mouths in anticipation of the forthcoming feast.

Ellie ground some of the few remaining coffee beans and set the coffee pot to boil on the fire. They would have a hot drink to accompany the cooked rabbit.

Finally, as chief cook, she cut a thin slice from the meat sizzling on the spit and divided it into three morsels, offering these to her companions. All declared the rabbit ready to be consumed, and they fell to demolishing the beast rapidly to a bare carcass, from which every scrap of edible meat had been devoured.

Washed down with a hot drink of coffee-flavoured water, the trio felt more than ready to face a long day's march towards their distant objective, the gold diggings at Casa Grande. As before, Josh was to range ahead in the hope of killing something for the pot with Gray Hawk's bow and one of the three remaining arrows, while Ellie and Ben would follow with the now lightly laden burro.

'Keep your eyes open for Apaches, lad. We haven't seen anything of those varmints, but something tells me they're around here. We're still in their territory!'

Josh agreed with Ben's observation as he forged ahead, and Ellie clutched the handle of her Smith and Wesson apprehensively, at the mere thought of encountering the Indians who had destroyed the people she had called family.

It was fortunate indeed that none of them knew what was taking place at the gathering at the far end of the valley they had just traversed.

CHAPTER 10

The word had gone out among The People. There was to be a Grand Council at the head of the valley, known in the Apache tongue as 'the place where water once flowed'. The various bands all sent their representatives to the meeting. Those present were, in the majority, Mescaleros and Chiricahuas, but there were also Lipan and White Mountain Apache, and even some of their distant cousins, the Navajo.

The council fire was lit, and the chief of the Mescaleros rose to address the gathering. The chief, Diablito, to give him his Spanish name, waited until he had silence, and then with his arms folded he looked around and finally spoke:

'My brothers. The People are an ancient and honorable people, but in recent times we have all fallen upon evil times. The strangers we call the White Eyes have appeared among us speaking with false tongues of friendship. They came from the South and we welcomed them as they passed through our land, but they did not treat us with respect, but hunted us down and even offered the things they call pesos in return for the scalps of Apache men, women and even children. Many of us have now been at war with these Mexicanos from the South for many moons – and now a new danger has arisen.

'More and more White Eyes of the Americano tribe have been entering our homeland. They build their wickiups, many of them, and say we, the Apache people, cannot enter these places they call towns. Others enter our hunting grounds and tell us that this is now their territory and we are forbidden to hunt there any more.

'More of the Americanos come seeking the yellow metal they call gold. They tear up the land despoiling the resting places of our ancestors, and now we learn that they are engaging in evil sacrifices of anyone who has the misfortune to fall into their hands.'

Diablito told the assembly in great detail the story of Little Buffalo's discovery of the corpse of Gray Hawk, and how the latter had undoubtedly been the victim of some diabolical sacrifice.

'We have determined that the perpetrators of this evil deed came from the place where the Ancient Ones had once, many, many moons ago, built their houses high up in the side of the cliffs for defence. And now the Americanos are gouging up the ground of the Ancient Ones in this mad desire for gold.

'I say enough is enough. Let us raise the war cry and drive these evil ones from the place they call Casa Grande. I, Diablito have spoken!'

Speaker after speaker stood up to support Diablito's

proposal, and it was agreed that a united effort be made to drive the Americanos from the place they called Casa Grande.

The day had been uneventful for the three travellers, cautiously making their way closer to where they confidently expected to locate the gold diggings of Casa Grande. At Josh's insistence they had kept away from the main trail, choosing instead to pick their way between the rocky outbreaks that littered the valley floor, which, though inconvenient, meant that for a good part of the journey they tended to be free from observation.

Josh could not have explained from whence came his desire for continued concealment. Certainly it was not the sentiment expressed by old Ben, who, earlier, would have agreed with the younger man. However, now that their march was drawing to a close he believed that Josh was being unduly careful, and told him so in no uncertain terms. Ellie, out of loyalty to the boy, kept silent, although in her heart she tended to agree with the old prospector.

So far Josh had not scared up any edible game that day, and that factor added to the grumbling coming from Ben as they made their way slowly towards their distant goal. Tired of the constant barrage of complaints coming from Ben, Josh was considering surrendering to the others' plea that they head towards the centre of the valley, when a loud noise claimed his attention.

Out towards the centre of the valley shots were

being fired, and seconds later, they heard triumphant war whoops that could only have come from the throats of Apache warriors. Smoke drifted skywards, there were more whoops, a distant thunder of horses' hoofs – and then silence.

Bidding his companions to remain in hiding, Josh made his way slowly and cautiously to the area from whence the sounds had come. He feared what he would discover, and his negative thoughts were confirmed as he carefully parted the brush that surrounded a gold miners' camp. A burnt tent and two white bodies stripped, but not otherwise mutilated, were lying on the ground in front of a still glowing campfire, while a pair of dead mules completed the slaughter caused by the raiding party.

Josh did not know that the attackers had acted alone. They had been summoned to the Council gathering, but had decided to have a little sport on the way. In doing so they had inadvertently given warning to the miners at Casa Grande that an Apache attack was possibly imminent. This was because a third miner, Vern Warran, had been absent from the camp, having gone some distance away to relieve himself; hearing the attack, he had wisely remained in hiding. When the Apaches left, he too departed, and fled towards the centre of the settlement, raising the alarm that an Apache attack could take place at any moment.

CHAPTER 11

Casa Grande, so called because of the ancient dwellings to be seen high above in the gouged-out hollow in the rocky side of the cliffs, was no frontier town. It wasn't even a frontier village. True, there was a well beaten track optimistically called Main Street, but the other tracks wandered haphazardly, with no attempt at order, or with any relationship to the above named.

Main Street consisted of a large tented saloon, The Lucky Nugget, while nearby was a half timber, half canvas establishment, The Emporium, where one could buy canned goods and many of the small products found in a general hardware store. There was a lean-to that was a combined Land and Assay Office, and another tented structure known as Mother Carey's, which catered for the carnal desires of the diggers. These four structures were the centre and focal point of Casa Grande.

For hundreds of yards all around, the land was dotted with holes and depressions and the makeshift dwellings of the would-be gophers, who optimistically sought to make their fortunes in the valley of the Casa Grande. Above, high on the cliffs, was the remarkably well preserved adobe building from which the site received its name. The Big House dominated the shoddy dwellings of the miners below.

When Vern Warran arrived, out of breath and hatless, crying that his comrades had been massacred, the word spread like wildfire of an impending attack by bloodthirsty savages. Main Street soon swarmed with dozens of wild-eyed miners, armed to the teeth, all milling around looking for a leader to direct their defence.

Ideas were brought forth and just as readily discarded. Build a barricade! What with? There was no lumber and little stone immediately nearby. Send to Fort Burnside for assistance from the cavalry detachment stationed there? It was twenty-five miles to the fort, and by the time a messenger reached there and relief arrived back at Casa Grande, they could all be dead and scalped! Could they negotiate with the Apache? Who could speak Apache? There was silence! No one came forth to offer their linguistic skills.

There was a common cry of 'Well, I'm not staying here to be massacred!' and a large number of the crowd stated their avowed intent of getting away to Fort Burnside. Others agreed, and very quickly two or three dozen miners had decided to band together and, believing in safety in numbers, to retreat through the mountains to the military fort.

Thus the population of Casa Grande divided into

two camps: those in favour of going to the fort, and those prepared to stay and fight. This latter group decided that The Emporium was the best structure that could be fortified, and they set to work, moving bales and boxes against the walls, and filling all available barrels and casks with water, in anticipation of a siege.

CHAPTER 12

Josh meanwhile had returned to the rocks where his companions were waiting. Before leaving the site of the murdered miners he had hurriedly checked their burnt tent for any foodstuffs that could be salvaged, and had obtained several cans, bags of flour and coffee together with a side of bacon, scorched along one side but still edible. Heavily laden with as much as he could carry, he found the hideout and dumped his findings on the ground as he gasped out the sorry tale of the dead men and the state of their camp.

'There was nothing that I could have done. The two men were dead and there was no time to bury them. I figured that we could use the food which otherwise would be left to rot, or stolen by more savages. As it is, I'm curious to know why they didn't loot the camp. It ain't like Indians to leave stuff around!'

Ben refused to be mollified by the sight of the victuals stacked before him. 'I guess you mean well young fella, but I just can't see the point of hanging around here hiding when we can be heading to where there's more of our folk.'

Josh shrugged his shoulders, 'Ben, I can't rightly tell you why I hesitate to go into Casa Grande! It's just something I feel, but I can't explain it. How about you, Ellie? What do you think?'

Ellie looked at Josh and spread her hands in a helpless gesture. 'I dunno, Josh. Somehow I think that maybe Ben is right. We wouldn't be in danger in Casa Grande among civilized people, but on the other hand, Josh, you have been right so often that I'm inclined to do whatever you decide.'

Josh turned back to Ben. 'I'm sorry, Ben! I guess Ellie and me'll have to stay out here a couple more days! If you want to go to Casa Grande right now, that's your choice. You can take some of the food with you, and of course Jacob, he's your burro. We'll miss you, but we can't stop you doing what you want to do.'

Old Ben shuffled his feet, and after looking back and forth between his two travelling companions, he bent down and picked out a can of beans, and hacked off a piece of bacon, saying, 'Well, I guess this'll do me 'til I get to town.' He packed a few belongings on the burro, and hesitantly bade Josh and Ellie farewell, saying: 'S'long kids! Come on Jacob! We're on our way to town!' And man and burro departed.

Josh stared out after the old miner as he and his little burro faded into the distance amid the cacti and yucca plants until they disappeared in a fold of the landscape. Then, with a shrug, he turned to Ellie saying, 'Ellie, it's just you and me again. I sure hope I'm doing the right thing!'

Ellie smiled, and after reassuring him of her faith in his judgment, being practical she got a small fire started and selected materials with which to cook supper. Josh, following her example, moved the supplies that he had obtained to a sheltered overhang, and set out several traps in the hope of catching more food. Both tried to keep busy, being conscious of the absence of their third partner.

Night fell on the valley of the Casa Grande. In their location among the rocks Josh and Ellie, having eaten their late supper, allowed the fire to die down, having banked it in the hope of having one or two coals still alight in the morning. They then curled up together and settled down to try and sleep.

Out in the valley Ben, having eaten cold beans and chewed on half-cooked bacon, also settled down with the satisfaction of knowing that he would buy a good meal in the morning when he reached town.

In town the 'stay behinders', as they called themselves, worked on through the night strengthening their defences, developing a series of rifle pits in front of the main barricades, and moving saloon stock into the store to reduce temptation on the part of defenders and attackers to indulge in strong liquor. Even the girls from Mother Carey's establishment were present, rolling impromptu bandages and preparing to undertake nursing duties.

On the trail to Fort Burnside the column of miners and their dependants sank wearily to the hard, unyielding ground, many already regretting the haste with which they had abandoned the diggings. A roster of sentry duties was arranged, and while some of the 'fort party' tried to cook basic meals for their supper, others, exhausted, closed their eyes and sought solace in sleep.

And at the head of the valley, hundreds of Apache warriors made their final preparations for the forthcoming attack, checking and re-checking their weaponry and applying war paint to both themselves and their ponies with extra care before participating in the great war dance around the council fire.

Diablito had been appointed War Chief of the assembled tribes. He was no great military strategist, but his objective was clear: namely, to rid the Valley of the Casa Grande of all accursed White Eyes. To achieve this objective he had proposed the following plan.

An advance band of about forty or fifty warriors would leave early, and by a little known trail, would set up an ambush on the path leading to the place known as Burnside's Fort. That should take care of any who escaped from the valley. The main party would sweep from the head of the valley towards the White Eyes settlement, not just along the main trail but also either side as far as the cliffs, killing any individuals or groups that they discovered. All would eventually gather for the main attack on the settlement. It was a simple plan, but should prove successful.

At sunrise all was ready. The advance party had departed hours before, and by that time should have been reaching their objective. Hundreds of warriors were milling around mounted on their paint-daubed ponies awaiting the signal. Diablito raised his lance, waving it around his head and finally pointing it down the valley. Shrill cries erupted from the throats of the assembled warriors as they surged forth like a mighty flood, spreading across the floor of the valley and raising clouds of dust as they rode.

CHAPTER 13

Josh and Ellie had arisen as the sun peeped over the tops of the eastern heights, with the former still agonizing over his irrational decision to remain away from all that represented civilization. The air was still as the hot sun rose higher. Then away towards the head of the valley there was a distant rumbling, as though a storm was on its way. But Josh thought this was very curious, as the sky was a deep blue, with none of the normal characteristics that usually heralded the onset of stormy weather. While Ellie fixed a simple meal, he climbed up on to the rocks that surrounded their clearing, and peered towards the head of the valley.

A clear view was obscured by clouds of dust, and he was startled to note that the dust cloud was advancing – and then, to his horror, Josh began to see the distant shapes of horsemen appearing and disappearing. It was like seeing an avalanche, a horizontal avalanche, that was coming closer with every second.

Josh slid down from the rocks, 'Quickly Ellie! Help me get all our supplies hidden among the rocks. There's no time to lose! Hurry!'

And Ellie, bewildered by the sudden turn of events, obeyed Josh's directions without question, stowing cans and sacks out of sight and helping to brush away footprints and other signs of their presence. Then the two of them crouched down with pistols drawn in a small cleft to await the passing of the human storm.

Ben Johnson struggled to his feet, ruefully rubbing his hips after a cold night attempting to sleep on ground that seemed to have got harder as he had grown older. 'Well Jacob! It's just a short journey for us this morning, and then you and I can have a long rest!' His burro looked up at the sound of Ben's voice and then, shaking his head from side to side, lowered it to resume grazing on the sparse foliage.

Then the rumble that Ben had thought was the far-off sound of a storm approaching, changed to the thunderous roar of hundreds of hoofs pounding the sandy soil, and clouds of dust boiled up, in the midst of which could be seen the terrifying sight of painted horses bearing painted warriors, all, it seemed, intent on riding him down.

Before the old prospector could take any further action the swiftly moving horde was upon them: clutching Jacob round the neck, both he and his burro received arrows that ended their existence – Ben's last mortal thought was, 'Damn! That wretched boy was right again!'

The miners and their dependants who made up the people heading for Fort Burnside, arose disgruntled with the glum thought that they had yet another day's trek and more before they could reach safety. With no acknowledged leader among them, there was little coordination as they started the second day's march, with the result that what was initially a compact body, rapidly became a mob straggling along the trail and spread out over a distance of half a mile.

And that is how the Apache ambush party found them. Suddenly the hapless miners found themselves under attack. The air was thick with arrows, many of which thudded into human flesh, while others ricocheted off the rocks and the hard surface of the trail. Amid the arrows were the isolated sounds of gunfire from the few Apache who possessed firearms, and also from the few White Eyes who had time to get their weapons into action. Lone warriors, seeking a name for themselves, would bound forwards into a group of fleeing whites with bloodcurdling shrieks and yells, tomahawk their selected victim, and just as rapidly spring back among the rocks. The trail to Fort Burnside would henceforth always be known as the 'Trail of Death'. Only five men and one woman reached the safety of the military post.

At The Emporium, sentries had noticed the dust clouds gathering further up the valley, and had alerted the little garrison of a probable attack. So they were standing by their posts with rifles and shotguns clenched in their hands, white-knuckled, when the Apache storm broke upon them.

Suddenly the hostile horsemen were all around the

fortified building, and the air was filled with a cloud of arrows thudding into the boxes and bales and the clap-board timbers that sheltered the defenders. Far too often an arrow would sink into the flesh of an exposed man or woman, as they attempted to aim their weapon at the Apache warriors hurtling past. Too often the brave, after loosing his arrow, would vanish from view as he rolled and clung to the far side of his steed.

Flesh wounds were treated, and the walking wounded returned to the firing line. If the arrow was too deeply embedded to be removed immediately, the afflicted one was made more or less comfortable in a central part of the one-time store, or was set to work rolling bandages or other useful tasks. The girls from Mother Carey's staggered from post to post with dixies full of water, offering some solace to the dry-throated defenders. Thus morning approached noon with the defences intact, but with an increasing number of incapacitated defenders.

Diablito was surprised, but not dismayed, by the stout resistance put up by the hated White Eyes. He was, however, concerned by the mounting Apache casual-ties resulting from the mounted attack, and he ordered a change of tactics. Warriors were to withdraw out of range, dismount and advance on foot, keeping under cover as much as possible, but gradually closing in on the White Eyes' position. When the time was right he intended to launch a frontal attack on all sides and overwhelm the defence with sheer numbers.

CHAPTER 14

Two miles away, hidden in their rocky outcrop, Josh and Ellie could hear the sounds of shooting, and also faintly detect the Apache yells carried on the wind. But they couldn't see anything of the battle that was being fought in the valley, leaving their imaginations to fear the worst.

'What are we going to do, Josh?' whispered Ellie, shivering at the thought of being captured and probably tortured by the raiders whom she could hear shrieking in the distance, and she clutched at Josh's arm in sheer panic, digging her nails into his flesh.

'I don't rightly know, Ellie!' muttered her companion, 'But if you don't stop ripping my arm to shreds, I'm going to clobber you, and I mean it! Let me think!' and he raised his free hand in a half jesting manner as though he would strike her if she didn't desist.

Ellie was immediately penitent. 'Sorry, Josh. It's just that I'm so scared!' She buried her head in the boy's shoulder, and he responded by putting an arm round her and hugging her tight.

'Brace up, Ellie! We'll get out of this mess, I promise you!' He continued to hold Ellie and shook her gently. 'You've proved that you're a tough girl so far, and we'll find some place where the Apache can't get us, you'll see. Now let's see you smile!'

Ellie lifted her head and presented a little half smile, half grimace, at which Josh grinned as he suggested that possibly they should try to find a safer hiding place.

Cautiously they emerged from among the rocks where they had been hiding. The siege at the settlement continued unabated, although by now it consisted of isolated firing in response to individual attacks. Josh looked around. The time must be past noon, as the sun had now cast the cliff behind them into deep shadow. They were immediately below the gigantic gash in the rocky surface, wherein were the adobe buildings that gave the valley its name: Casa Grande. Was there any way up to the ledge and the adobe dwellings there?

Josh scanned the rock face slowly and carefully. Yes! If he looked at a certain angle a series of depressions could be seen in the rock, depicting a perilous ascent up to the ledge. Excitedly, Josh turned to the girl at his side.

'Look, Ellie! Up there is the place where we would be safe. It would take courage to make the climb, but we can do it!'

Ellie's eyes followed his pointing finger, and she turned to him in horror. 'Josh Martin! You surely don't expect me to climb that, do you? You must be crazy!'

Josh had expected resistance to his plan, and offered the girl the alternatives. She could remain below and risk discovery by the Apaches. They could attempt to join the besieged people holding out in the settlement, but there wasn't any certainty that they would get there, nor that the defenders would be successful in holding their position. Or they could attempt the climb. If they reached the ledge they would be safe. The climb wasn't half as bad as the one he had made down to the wrecked stagecoach.

Josh clinched the argument by suggesting that, if Ellie was adamant in her decision to remain below, he would climb alone to the ledge and she could remain where she was and, hopefully, would not be discovered by any searching hostiles. But at the thought of being by herself once more Ellie reluctantly agreed to try and make the climb, and together they moved their small store of supplies to the foot of the cliff where the footholds began.

From where they stood there was a rocky slope, indicating where the ancient cliff dwellers had dumped unwanted rock, stone, smashed adobe material and broken pottery down to the outcrop where they had first found sanctuary. Ellie and Josh, at the summit of the pile, looked up at the rock face in dark shadow compared with the glaring sunlight below.

The footholds and the corresponding handholds could be clearly seen when viewed at a certain angle, and Josh gave Ellie some final instructions. 'Listen carefully. I'll go first. Then I'll lower the lariat and haul up the other canteens and our food. Then finally, Ellie, I want you to tie a bowline, you know how to do it, around your body and climb up. I'll keep the lariat fairly tense so you'll be quite safe!'

Taking one of the three canteens they possessed, and the long length of rawhide lariat left by Ben coiled over his shoulder, Josh tackled the climb, leaving Ellie standing staring fearfully at his ascending form, with one hand pressed against her mouth constantly whispering, 'Take care, Josh! Oh, do be careful!'

Josh climbed slowly and carefully, brushing aside the accumulations of dirt, sand and God knows what from each foothold before testing it gingerly and then transferring his weight on to it. There were no mishaps, and finally Josh thankfully pulled himself on to the ledge of the Casa Grande.

Quickly he uncoiled the lariat, and securing one end to a convenient block of stone, which no doubt had been employed in a similar manner by the original inhabitants, he lowered the line down to Ellie. There was just enough, with possibly three feet to spare, and Ellie set to work.

The other two canteens made up the first load, and having secured them, she signalled to Josh to haul away. He did so, and rapidly brought their water supply up to his position. The food supplies followed, together with the coffee pot and frying pan, and the weapons that had belonged to the dead Apache.

While doing her tasks Ellie tried deliberately not to think about the last load that would have to be raised, or rather assisted up those awful cliffs. Namely herself!

In truth she was absolutely terrified at the prospect, and having a healthy imagination, dwelt on many of the potential disasters that could befall her. She could slip. She lacked the strength to pull herself up a cliff face. The lariat would break. The fall wouldn't kill her, but would leave her paralysed and helpless. Josh hated her, making her perform this dreadful thing.

The last remaining load vanished up the cliff, and the lariat came snaking down. Ellie stood there trembling, holding the end of the line as though bewitched. Josh's voice came from above: 'Come on Ellie! I know you can do it!'

There was no response. Ellie remained rooted in the one spot. Josh leaned out and peered down. There was no movement from the girl below. He knew that he had to shock her into action. 'Ellie, quickly! There are four Apaches down among the rocks. They're searching and getting closer. Hurry now, there's no time to lose!' – and Ellie, spurred into action, passed the lariat around herself under the armpits and rapidly made a bowline, tugging to her companion to take up the slack. Josh did so, and Ellie commenced to climb.

As she did so, her fears diminished as she concentrated on seeking out the hand- and footholds ahead of her, thankful for the fact that Josh never allowed the lariat to become slack, and therefore she had this constant pressure drawing her ever upwards. It seemed but a short while before she was pulling herself up on to the ledge of the Casa Grande and facing a grinning Josh, who patted her on the back, declaring: 'Well done, Ellie! I knew you could do it!'

Breathless, Ellie smiled back at him, then turned and peered out across the valley. 'Josh! Where are the Apaches that you saw?' she queried in a puzzled tone.

Josh responded in an off-hand tone: 'Oh, I guess they've decided to look elsewhere, or maybe they've gone back and joined their buddies fighting around the settlement.'

Ellie pursed her lips and stared at him accusingly. 'Josh Martin, you lying beast! I don't think there were any Indians nearby! I think you just wanted to scare me so that you could have your own way. I'll never talk to you again!' So saying, she stalked off to another part of the ledge and plonked herself down, hugging her knees and staring out across the valley as tears gathered in her eyes.

Josh wisely remained silent, figuring that it would be best to let Ellie work her anger out of her system. Meanwhile, he too gazed with great interest at the scene spread out below. From where he sat he could clearly see in the far distance the white outline of the tent, which still partially covered the general store where the white people were forted up, and from which there came, at irregular intervals, puffs of white smoke, followed belatedly by the far-off boom of the defenders' long guns. He was also in a position to observe the activities of the Apache attackers, as the ant-like figures scurried from place to place and, periodically, could be seen to rush forwards and then retreat, leaving the odd person motionless.

Switching his gaze to the near side of the valley, isolated figures of natives could be seen checking the abandoned locations where the miners had been at work, and no doubt looting any articles that took their primitive fancy. He saw that indeed there were also searchers moving closer to where he and Ellie had originally hidden, and realizing that any Apache looking up would be able to detect them sitting on the brink of the ledge above, moved back and called upon Ellie to do the same.

'Ellie! I think we had better get back from the cliff edge so those Apache down there don't see us.'

Startled by Josh's remark, Ellie emerged from her trance-like state and looked down, and on seeing the Apache warriors moving purposefully among the rocks below, hurriedly left her exposed position and crept over to where Josh was sitting. Seating herself close, she slipped out a little hand, and finding his, held it, whispering; 'Josh, I'm sorry I got so angry at you! I didn't mean what I said. You know that, don't you?'

Josh's response was to give her a hug and, raising his left hand to his mouth, he placed one finger across his lips muttering, 'Shush!'

Motioning for Ellie to follow him, he moved along the ledge through the ruined adobe dwellings to the far end, where, cautiously approaching the edge of the cliff, he could look diagonally down to where they had made their ascent.

There were several warriors to be seen searching every cleft and hollow amid the rocky surface that might have provided refuge for any would-be fugitives, and the two White Eyes, peering down on the scene from above, were thankful that they had made the climb, and with luck, would remain hidden from their enemies.

One brave called to his fellows and they moved away, obviously intent on rejoining the main war band still besieging the store-house building of the white intruders in the valley of the Casa Grande.

Ellie and Josh breathed a sigh of relief as the Apaches departed, and Josh indicated that they could at last explore their new domain and set up camp. Hand in hand they made a complete survey of the ledge-top adobe ruins, curious to see how primitive people could have chosen such a strange location in which to set up house.

The ledge on which they were standing was a cavity in the face of the cliff, which formed their side of the valley. The cavity was approximately three hundred feet in length, with a slight incline from one end to the other, no doubt following the strata of the rock formation. The ledge extended close on thirty feet back from the edge, and had a ceiling which in most cases was a good fifteen feet above the point where they were standing.

This, then, was the strange location in which the long-dead natives of the valley had chosen to construct their adobe dwellings, now a series of roofless and crumbling walls, yet with enough remaining to give the valley its Spanish name of Casa Grande: the Big House.

Josh and Ellie were delighted to locate, hidden away in the back of the cavern, water seeping down into a natural basin: this had been enlarged by the original inhabitants, who had led the overflow away to drain down into the rock. Another area, where the rocky ceiling was blackened with the smoke from countless fires, suggested a place where cooking had taken place, and where there was a fissure available to act as a natural chimney. This prompted Ellie to scavenge among the adobe buildings, seeking wood from collapsed roofing material, then to build a fire and cook them both a hearty meal of bacon, beans and twist bread, washed down with several cups of coffee.

While Ellie was engaged in her culinary skills, Josh had not been idle. Being very aware of the fact that they could receive unwelcome visitors at any time, he had set to work gathering large pieces of rock that had fallen from the roof of the cavern, and chunks of adobe bricks, piling them close to where the crude stairway reached the ledge. He figured that a deluge of rock and brick could well persuade any attackers to depart and leave them in peace. He had heard that most Indians did not engage in night fighting, but not being sure that the Apaches were of this persuasion, he decided that they would have to take turns being on guard duty.

These matters were discussed with his female companion after supper, and apart from pulling a little face at the thought of having a broken night's rest, Ellie agreed with Josh's plan. So, leaving the boy on guard, she curled up to try and sleep.

Josh was wide awake as night fell on the valley, and

he stared out and across to the now silent settlement, wondering how the defenders had fared during the day-long fighting.

CHAPTER 15

Down in the Emporium filthy, smoke-blackened men and women slumped down exhausted behind their arrow-studded barricades, in many cases too tired to consume the limited food brought to them by Mother Carey's young 'ladies'. However, they grasped greedily at cups of water in an attempt to slake their thirst, which had been exacerbated by the day-long task of tearing open with their teeth the paper cartridges used to load their muzzle-loading rifles.

The attacks had tapered off as the sun sank in the western sky, and silently the people hoped that they would get a brief respite from conflict during the hours of darkness. The fainthearted among the defenders suggested the possibility of buying off the Apache, but were swiftly ordered to keep such thoughts to themselves as there was to be no thought of any form of surrender. Thus the night passed in an encampment which, due to the limited facilities, was rapidly becoming unpleasant, with the groans of the wounded, coupled with the odour of sweat-laden bodies, and smells that arose from the fact that nobody had considered the need for people to relieve themselves while cooped up in such a cramped space.

Meanwhile the six survivors of the Trail of Death had staggered the remaining distance to Fort Burnside and poured out their tragic story to the officer commanding at the post. He, with a limited garrison of a half company of infantry under his command, could not leave the fort unmanned while attempting the rescue of the people left at Casa Grande, and sent frantic messages by heliograph to General Percivale at Fort Scott. Unfortunately, until the sun rose the following morning, the heliographic mode of communication was inoperable.

Diablito stalked from one group of Apache warriors to another, sensing their dismay at not securing a swift victory over the White Eyes, and endeavouring to rouse their spirits by praising the valour of each man, reminding them of the reason why they were engaged in this war.

One small group of braves had been engaged in serious debate most of the evening. They had been searching the rocky area over towards the cliff face, below where the ancient ones had built their houses, and a couple of the men believed they may have overlooked something. They persuaded their companions that if the siege of the White Eyes' camp continued through the next day, they should resume their search of the area where they had left off the previous day.

*

Dawn came as the sun rose into a clear blue sky. Up in their aerie Ellie, having taken over guard duty in the early hours of the morning, busied herself with starting a fire and boiling the pot full of water, to allow herself a small quantity for washing and sufficient to make coffee. With a fond glance at her sleeping companion, she decided to let Josh continue slumbering since he had remained awake for the better part of the night.

At Fort Scott, General Percivale did what he had been doing most of his adult life: he passed the buck. That is, he telegraphed Washington reporting the situation, then awaited further instructions. The reply came back immediately.

'Take whatever troops are available and march to the relief of the people at Casa Grande.' There was, however, a second message: 'Negotiate with hostiles to clear all white people from the valley.'

Gratified that the decision to mount an expeditionary force had been made by one senior to himself, General Percivale ordered the Fourth Cavalry Regiment to parade ready to march, every man to carry one hundred rounds of ammunition, filled canteens and four days' emergency rations. More ammunition and supplies were to be carried with two mountain howitzers that were to accompany the column.

A message was immediately heliographed to Fort

Burnside: 'We're on our way!' and the military machine swung into action.

With the men riding at attention, the regiment, henceforth to be known as the 'Saviours of Casa Grande', rode jauntily through the gateway of Fort Scott with the regimental band playing a spirited air, General Percivale taking the salute, and the regimental wives waving handkerchiefs and silently praying that their men might return safely.

Dawn had brought no pleasure to the men and women cooped up in the fortified enclosure they were now calling Fort Emporium. With daybreak, the sniping had resumed in intensity, and also the volume of arrows delivered by the besieging Apaches – but fortunately, there were no further white casualties. Food was issued in small but adequate quantities, and likewise, watered coffee laced with rum from the stores of the now demolished saloon.

Somebody suggested that periodically the defenders should sing, partly to raise their own spirits, but also as an act of defiance to show the Indians that the White Eyes were not downhearted. Shortly thereafter, the warbling sound of 'My Darling Clementine' could be heard rising from the encampment, to the puzzlement of the Apaches, many of whom, optimistically, thought that the Whites were singing their death song.

CHAPTER 16

Ellie had soaked some dried beans overnight, and she now fried these with a few scraps of bacon for flavouring and a pinch of flour to thicken the sauce. When the beans were browning, she decided that it was time to awaken Josh – but first she took a quick peep over the edge of the ledge to ensure all was well. To her dismay there were at least a dozen Apache braves moving among the rocks, searching as they came, but appearing to be moving purposefully towards the cliff. Ellie rushed over to where Josh lay curled up, sleeping with his head cushioned on one arm. She shook the boy frantically, whispering: 'Josh! Josh! Wake up! I think there's a war party below and they're approaching the place where we climbed the cliff!'

Josh sat up and shook his head groggily as he attempted to collect his thoughts. 'Wassa matter Ellie? Did you say Apaches? Where?' and he looked around in bewilderment.

Then he suddenly grasped the full intent of Ellie's muted cry, and crawling over to the edge, he peered down. Ellie had spoken truly. Below, right at the cliff face, there was gathered a knot of heavily armed

Indians talking excitedly among themselves with one pointing at the rocky surface before them. Suddenly he pointed his arm upwards, and eleven Indian heads followed the movement.

None too soon Josh jerked his head back, and once out of view, trotted further along the ledge to where he could once more see what was happening below with less fear of discovery.

If he could have eavesdropped on his enemies and understood their language, he would have learned that they were divided into two camps. One group, led by a young, muscular brave, was excitedly attempting to persuade his fellows that they must climb the cliff and search the adobes above. An older warrior with wrinkled visage was declaring that such a course was sacrilege, and that it could well bring the wrath of the Ancient Ones down upon them. His argument was countered by that of a third, who declared that if the White Eyes had climbed up to the Casa Grande, then it was they who had first committed sacrilege, and that therefore the evil would fall upon them first. The quasi-theological discussion continued for some time until finally, those in favour of searching above won the day: led by the stocky one, they made preparations for the climb.

Josh returned to his original position where, bolting down the food offered to him by a shaking Ellie and hurriedly drinking a cup of coffee, he prepared to repel the invaders. Picking up a piece of rock the size of a large loaf of bread, he held it at the cliff edge and then, chancing a quick glance below, gently slid the missile beyond the point of balance and let go.

Young Bull, satisfied that he had won the argument in favour of climbing to the cliff dwellings, had placed his cherished rifle on the ground and, slinging his bow across his back, commenced the climb up the cliff. He had hardly commenced his ascent when a large rock hurtled past him, and it was his ill luck that it landed on his firearm, breaking the stock at the small of the butt.

Shaken, he dropped down and angrily picked up his broken rifle, flourishing the two pieces as he looked up and shouted his defiance at the dwellings above. 'You above! I don't care if you are man or ghost, I am coming to get you! I, Young Bull, have spoken!'

His companions had drawn back when the rock came from above, and they now stared almost fearfully as Young Bull, dropping his broken gun, rushed towards the cliff and started making his way rapidly upwards.

Josh pushed a shower of broken pieces of adobe over the cliff, and Young Bull was suddenly engulfed in a deluge of whole and partial bricks, which struck him on the head and shoulders, causing him to huddle motionless against the cliff long after the strange shower had ceased.

Ellie meanwhile had boiled a coffee pot full of water with the intent of cleaning up their breakfast dishes, but remembering something she had once read in a book about sieges and castles in Europe, she offered the liquid to Josh.

Josh, smiling at her contribution, took the pot and,

stretching out his right arm and aiming carefully, poured a steady stream of boiling water down in the direction of the Apache, who had once more commenced his upward climb.

Young Bull, recovering from the adobe attack, was making good progress upwards when there was a warning shout from one of his comrades below, watching his ascent with great interest. He looked up and instinctively closed his eyes just in time, as he was struck by the countless droplets of boiling hot water that splashed on to his face, shoulders and outstretched arms. The result was catastrophic: scalded and feeling as though he were covered by a million fire ants, with an involuntary cry of agony he dropped to the rocky surface below, landing heavily and breaking his right femur in the process.

All day long the strange siege continued. Undeterred by the mishap that had befallen Young Bull, other Apache braves in turn attempted to reach the cliff dwellings – and all were defeated. Various stratagems were adopted by each attacker as they tried to climb the cliff. One sought to have the defender above blinded during his ascent by having a series of bowmen fire upwards at any cliff-top movement, so that Josh would not know exactly when to drop his missiles.

However, the White Eyes couple had prepared for such a situation. Ellie went along the cliff to the far end, from where she could safely look down diagonally, out of range of those below but able to observe any climbing attempts. She could then signal to Josh, and when appropriate he would immediately start pushing rocks and other debris down upon the head or heads of any climbers.

Another tied a rawhide shield to his back, hopefully to ward off the cascade of adobe debris that plunged down upon every would-be climber. Unwittingly he was emulating earlier warriors in history who had employed similar methods to try and achieve assaults on castle walls. In this particular case, Josh was forced to expend two of his precious pistol loads, and the ambitious climber found that his shield was no defence against .44 calibre lead bullets.

Young Bull, the first casualty, was carried back to the main encampment where the siege of Fort Emporium continued unabated, though with decidedly less enthusiasm. Siege warfare was not the Apache notion of battle, and many of the warriors were impatient with the idea of staring at a barricade for hours in the hope of seeing a momentary target in the shape of one of the White Eyes.

Therefore, upon learning of the alternative fight going on across the valley, they would slip away from their appointed post and make their way to where they, in turn, could try their luck at capturing the Casa Grande. As a result, as time went by, the number of warriors with broken limbs being carried back to Diablito's camp mounted.

Ellie and Josh were exhausted with the day's proceedings. Ellie kept the fire going and boiled water for use as a weapon, in addition to the task of fixing a makeshift meal for them to eat between onslaughts, and running back and forth acting as observer for Josh in his daylong battle. On one occasion, when an energetic warrior had made very fast progress up the cliff face at a moment when Josh's supply of missiles at hand was low, Ellie saved the day by scooping up hot coals in the frying pan and pouring them down upon the attacker, causing him to lose his grip and fall, with dire results.

During a lull between would-be attackers, Josh spent his time carrying and stacking more rocks and adobe bricks in preparation for the next attempt. Wiping his face and thankfully gulping down mugfuls of cool water brought for him by his willing helpmate, Josh's mind flashed back to the little schoolhouse in Indiana where he had received his scant education. Their teacher, an elderly crippled ex-soldier, had at times told his restless charges various stories in an attempt to stimulate their interest in learning to read. One tale in particular had made an impression on Josh, and now, during this period of extreme danger, he remembered the details vividly of how a single soldier, Horatio, had held attacking enemies at bay, on a bridge in ancient Rome, while his comrades dismantled the structure behind him.

'Well, I ain't no ancient Roman and my name certainly isn't Horatio, but no darned Apache is going to get up that stairway if I can help it,' thought Josh to himself as, after a quick peep over the edge, he dropped several large pieces of brick down upon a warrior half way up the cliff: as was his intention, the latter fell to the rocks below.

Gradually, as the afternoon passed and turned into evening, the cliff-scaling attempts diminished and Josh and Ellie had time to take stock of their situation. It was fairly evident that, as long as they had a supply of missiles and the time and energy to deliver them, they could hold their position, assuming they had enough food to sustain them in their struggle. Ellie, after a swift check of the supply situation, assured Josh that with care she could eke out the food to last them a full week. By the end of that time the situation would hopefully have improved.

CHAPTER 17

Meanwhile, the fight at the cliff face had not gone completely unnoticed. Someone in the garrison of Fort Emporium had noticed the trickle of Apache warriors making their way over to the far cliffs, and with a pair of Swiss binoculars was able to see the ant-sized figures attempting to scale the rock face to the cliff dwellings; he made the correct assumption that they were trying to overcome some opposition there.

In the Emporium there was now an air of optimism. The Apache attacks had abated considerably and there had been no further casualties. Those wounded during the initial attacks seemed to be responding to the rough and ready treatment available, and all were greatly cheered by the news that elsewhere in the valley, folks appeared to be successfully resisting the Apache onslaught.

In the meantime, the Fourth Cavalry had reached Fort Burnside. Sending out scouts every foot of the way and proceeding extremely cautiously, General Percivale had ponderously brought his column to a point where a lightning strike could bring them to the relief of the garrison of the beleaguered post. It was not to be! Darkness was approaching, and General Percivale, having listened carefully to the horrible tales of the six survivors of the trail of death, was determined that his men would not be caught in a similar trap. They would wait until morning and then advance.

The next morning, after a quiet night and a decent early breakfast, both Josh and Ellie felt remarkably confident as they faced the thought of still more Apache warriors attempting the cliff-face climb under a hail of their rock and adobe missiles. As the first warrior of the day approached the place where the foot- and handholds commenced, Josh tentatively dropped a single brick, which hit the ground and shattered, sending up a small cloud of dust and fragments, no more than a foot away from the would-be climber's feet – whereupon the Apache warrior shook his head and turned away, deciding that this challenge was too much for him.

In Fort Emporium that morning there was guarded optimism that they were winning the battle against the native warriors. There had been no early morning attacks launched against the defences, and apart from the occasional arrow or rifle shot fired towards the barricades, there was little activity to indicate that the hostiles were still present. In fact the worst aspect of the siege were the abysmal living conditions to which the defenders were subjected, and the throat-gagging odour that pervaded the atmosphere, plus the count-less flies drawn to the location by the unburied dead and excrement.

At Fort Burnside all was ready for the advance. Reveille had been at five o'clock, with the bugle call of 'Boots and Saddles' at six-thirty – and then the regiment waited, with the men standing at ease by their horses, while General Percivale held an 'orders' meeting with his senior officers. Finally, the orders came that the regiment would advance, but only after the two moun-tain howitzers laid down a curtain of fire along the trail, behind which the cavalry would move forwards.

And so, to the periodic booms of exploding shells, the Fourth Cavalry advanced along the mountain trail that led to the valley of the Casa Grande. The move forwards was without incident, as the Apaches who had participated in the ambush of the White Eyes who had fled from the valley, had long since departed and returned to rejoin the main band. The only effect of the continuous shellfire was the further dismember-ment of the victims of the massacre already ravaged by vultures and other scavengers.

All morning long in Fort Emporium the level of excitement had been rising as the garrison listened to the far-off sound of gunfire, which, like the rumble of a summer storm, was seen to be gradually approaching as the noise increased in its intensity. It was obvious that relief was on its way, and men started slapping each other on the back, while periodically, others cheered at every explosion. By mid-morning, columns of black smoke could be seen following the detonation of each explosion, and the excitement of the beleaguered White Eyes rose accordingly.

Diablito was finding it increasingly difficult to control the warriors under his command. The more cautious among them advised a general withdrawal further up the valley, while the younger, more hot-headed braves, drunk with their success so far, called upon their war chief to lead them against the Pony Soldiers reported by scouts to be entering the valley.

Up in the cliff dwelling Josh and Ellie, from their elevated height, were in a position to actually observe the far-off effect as the shellfire began to enter the valley. The boom as a shell left the barrel was followed almost immediately by a flash of light as the missile exploded, followed by the smoke and sandy soil rising heavenwards as each projectile tore a shallow hole in the surface of the valley. It was apparent that delivery was close at hand. No enemy had attempted to climb the cliff face, and boy and girl clutched at each other excitedly as the group of Apaches slipped away from beneath them and made tracks to join their companions near the whites' settlement. Faced with the thought of leaving their refuge, Ellie cooked a meal with double rations, after which they sat replete, watching the scene below as though in a box of some gigantic opera house.

CHAPTER 18

Upon entering the valley the artillery bombardment had ceased as the cavalry emerged from the defile that had limited their movements, and now they spread out as a blue tide of men and horses on either side of the track before advancing towards the distant settlement. Then the cavalry halted, and a party carrying large white flags broke free from the centre and cantered down the trail leading to the settlement.

Ellie and Josh looked at each other, puzzled as to the activities. The former wrinkled her brow in bewilderment declaring; 'What does it all mean, Josh? Surely white flags are indicating that they want to surrender? That can't be right!'

'No, Ellie. I believe that the army wants to talk with the Apaches. I think they call it a parley. At least, I guess that's what it's all about.'

The parley party halted, and one distant figure, wearing buckskins rather than army blue, rode on alone and halted with both arms raised, showing that he was not carrying any weapon. Ellie and Josh were both decidedly curious as to what was happening below, and wished that they could somehow hear what was going on.

Clint Boykin, the army scout the two cliff dwellers were watching, was wishing that he had kept his mouth shut. An elderly man with scant grey hair now hidden under a battered old sombrero, Clint's leathery features were continually in motion as he repeatedly masticated on a large wad of well-chewed tobacco, while he reviewed the circumstances that had brought him to this unenviable position.

He had been sitting with Charley Bates while the column rested, yarning about the lack of beaver that year, when a young shave-tail lieutenant appeared, asking if anyone had a knowledge of the Apache language. Charley, blast him, had pointed a grubby finger at his pal and stated: 'Here's yer man, Lootenant! Speaks it like a native, 'e does!' And Clint, with a sudden surge of ego, had admitted that such was the case, omitting to say that his alma mater in this matter had been the bed of a young Mescalero widow whom he had comforted for a whole winter.

The 'shave-tail' had taken Clint before General Percivale, who had instructed him to go forwards with the 'parley' squad, to try to arrange a truce and a meeting with the chiefs of the Apaches. And here he was, riding out alone, quaking at the thought of all those hidden bows and rifles no doubt aimed at him, and that it only needed one shot from either a foolish trooper or an ambitious Indian for his body to become a human pincushion.

Diablito was curious. The entry of the Pony Soldiers into the valley had been reported to him, and of course he had heard the sound of the big guns on wheels, and knew that his warriors could not stand against such awesome power. Why then had the White Chief called for a parley? Was it a trap?

When the knowledge that the scout who rode ahead was Boykin, with whom he was quite familiar, he decided to at least listen to what the White Eye had to say. He therefore ordered that Clint Boykin be brought before him.

Apprehensively, Clint edged his horse forwards and followed the brave who took him to where Diablito and the other Apache chiefs waited. A long silence followed. Clint, outwardly nervous, swallowed his tobacco wad in an effort to remain calm. Diablito stared at him impassively. Finally he broke the silence. 'I see you, Boykin. Do you come to sell us more bad fire-water?'

'Now that was not my fault, Diablito! How did I know some dirty dog had switched the whiskey keg on me? I was tricked! No chief, the General sent me to invite you to a parley. I think he wants to make peace between the Apache nation and the White Eyes.'

Diablito turned to his fellow chiefs and translated the invitation. He had already come to the realization that they were not going to defeat the White Eyes holding out in the valley, and the appearance of hundreds of Pony Soldiers and the guns that tore up the ground convinced him that to continue fighting this war was a mistake. It did not take too much talking to

112

obtain unanimous support for the idea of meeting with General Percivale.

Josh and Ellie, seated high above the valley floor, were in a state of frustrated excitement. They had seen the tiny figure of an army scout move forwards, seen him disappear into a fold of the ground and, after a considerable length of time, had seen him reappear, riding fast to rejoin the parley squad who had also turned back to return to the main column. Shortly after that, a party of Apache, whose ceremonial attire was invisible to the distant watchers, rode sedately down the track towards the blue-coated military array. What was happening?

CHAPTER 19

The Apache chiefs halted in a bunch about twenty-five feet away from where General Percivale, his staff officers and orderlies waited. Diablito rode forwards, to be joined by Clint Boykin the scout. The General, not knowing that Diablito understood English, told Boykin to inform the Apache chief that he welcomed the opportunity to make peace with the Great Apache Nation, that there had been a grave misunderstanding, and that the white people in the valley of the Casa Grande were innocent farmers, who just wanted to live in peace beside their red brothers.

However, mindful of the instructions from Washington, he went on to say that if there had been any kind of offence, he, General Percivale, was there to make amends and ensure that all was harmonious in the whole region. The sincerity of his statements was rendered doubtful by his closing remark to Clint. 'Boykin, tell the old buzzard anything you like just so I can get off this damned horse. I have a severe medical problem that needs immediate attention, and I don't want to spend a minute longer in the saddle than I have to. Though don't tell him that, of course!'

To the General's astonishment and embarrassment, Diablito responded sarcastically to his remarks in clear but guttural English. 'General Percivale! We thank you for trying to solve this problem that has come between our two peoples, and I'm sorry that you have pain when sitting on your horse. Many old men have this problem.' The General wriggled uncomfortably.

'We are an ancient people who have lived among these mountains for many hundreds of years. When the Spanish people under Coronado came among us we welcomed them, but they tried to rob us because of the yellow metal you call gold. Then you American White Eyes came in much greater numbers for the same purpose, and you would drive us from our valleys and from places that are holy to us. This place, where the people who came before us lived, is what you would call . . .' Diablito paused, searching for the correct word, then continued '. . . It is sacred to us because the Old Ones lived and died and were buried in this valley. And now you people come and dig up the ground where our ancestors lived. We, the Apache, say, go from this place!'

The negotiations continued for a long time, but were in fact one-sided. The Apache chiefs stated their position through Diablito, and would not be budged. The White Eyes must dismantle their settlement and remove themselves, and all of their belongings, from the valley, which in future would be banned to white settlers. Once all had been removed, the Army should establish a small post at the entrance to the valley of the Casa Grande to bar any would-be trespassers. Diablito proposed that one White Eye, namely Clint Boykin, should reside with the Apache to act as the white representative.

General Percivale, becoming more and more uncomfortable with every minute, agreed with alacrity to every proposal, just so that he could get off his horse. The aides with him knew of his discomfort, as did the troopers of the escort – and before long, the results of the negotiations were known privately far and wide as the Treaty of Percivale's Butt.

The treaty was all drawn up for General Percivale to sign, and for the Apache chiefs to affix their marks, when Diablito stated: 'There is one more thing, General! All the people who are at this moment living up in the Casa Grande: they, too, must depart from this place!'

The news of the treaty and the conditions it contained filled the defenders of Fort Emporium with dismay when the description of the agreement reached them, and there were angry comments and blistering descriptions regarding General Percivale and his ancestry. Most of the defenders thought that they had been in a position to win the fight against the Apache, and the relieving troopers were startled to find that they received the brunt of the settlers' anger when, finally, the cavalry took up positions around the primitive fort to become a buffer between the inhabitants and the besieging natives.

Reluctantly, the inhabitants of Fort Emporium

started to dismantle their barricades, and, assisted by work parties of soldiers, to make wagons and carts serviceable for their departure from the valley, watched at a distance by groups of elated Apache braves.

CHAPTER 20

Up in the Casa Grande, Ellie and Josh had watched with great interest and no little excitement as in the distance the meeting between soldiers and Indians took place, and the subsequent advance of the cavalry to the isolated settlement. Ellie turned to Josh and suggested that perhaps they should go down and make their way to where the Army was now in command of the situation – but Josh shook his head.

'Not yet, Ellie. Look! The whole countryside between us and them soldiers is still crawling with Apaches and we'd never get through. We'll just have to wait and see if the Indians are forced to pull back, and then we'll see if we can get through. Be patient, Ellie!'

The girl made a little mew of discontent, but sat and hoped for an improvement in the scene below. In fact she didn't have long to wait, as shortly thereafter a large party of troopers could be seen making their way across the valley, with the Apaches melting away before them. Reaching the rocky area near to the side of the cliff, a dozen dismounted and proceeded closer on foot, leaving a small group to look after the horses. Reaching the cliff face, one, obviously an officer, called up to the white faces he could see looking down at him.

'Hello, up there! I'm Lieutenant Groves. Fourth Cavalry. I have orders from General Percivale to escort you all to our regimental headquarters after you evacuate your position up there. So, all of you come down. It's quite safe!'

There was a short silence, and then a young female voice replied; 'We're coming, Lieutenant! Just getting our stuff together!'

Moments later a bundle was lowered to the ground and when untied the line was raised and after a pause it reappeared fastened to an unkempt female who climbed down the cliff face, steadied in her progress by the same lariat.

She reached the rocky ground, and ignoring the troopers who hastened forwards to her assistance, called out: 'I'm down, Josh! Your turn now!'

A male figure swung himself over the edge above and swiftly made his way down, jumping the last few feet and turning to stand grinning at the officer and the troopers: 'Hiya fellas! It sure is good to see more white folks around here.'

The troopers crowded around slapping Josh on the back and shaking hands with Ellie, who was delighted with all this sudden attention. Lieutenant Groves, feeling that his authority was rapidly slipping away, called for silence; forgetting that he was probably only a year or two older than the boy he addressed, he then asked: 'Now, young man! Where are all the other men defending that building up there? We want everyone down here, now!'

Josh, somewhat irritated by Lieutenant Groves' attitude, which he decided was both arrogant and belittling, bristled at the way the young officer addressed him, and replied, 'Well mister! If you think there are more people up there, you'd better get up there yourself and get them down!' and he stared at the lieutenant defiantly, challenging him to make the climb, while some of the troopers openly chuckled at the shave-tail's discomfort.

Ellie, impressed at the manner in which Josh stood up to the cavalry officer, decided that it was time for her to intervene: 'Josh is right, Lieutenant. Him and me were the only folks up there. Are you calling us liars?'

Lieutenant Groves was taken aback. This was becoming ridiculous, and he looked around for a solution. 'You there, Trooper Muller! You're an athletic fella. Get up there and verify this young man's story!' Muller shrugged his shoulders, and in compliance with the order, slowly removed his belted pistol, holster and jacket; he then turned to Josh and asked: 'Any advice, friend, on going up this doggone stairway?'

Josh smiled encouragingly at him. 'Yes! Two things! Test every foot- and handhold before you put your weight on it, and secondly, don't look down!'

Trooper Muller shook hands with Josh, grinned at his comrades, and winked at Ellie; then he turned to the officer, stood rigidly at attention and asked formally: 'Permission to commence climbing, Sir?'

Silently Lieutenant Groves nodded and the cavalry trooper started to climb, watched with great interest by all present. Initially Muller's efforts were met with ribald cheers as he ascended, and with groans and boos every time his boots slipped – but Josh put a stop to their comments, negative or otherwise, stressing that what their comrade was attempting was a life and death endeavour, and that they were actually putting his life in greater danger by distracting him with their catcalls.

Thereafter they watched without comment as Muller steadily climbed up the primitive stairway, reached the top and hauled himself over the cliff edge and on to the ledge. He disappeared, and for a good ten minutes all below waited for the results of his search. At length Muller's head appeared once more, and he called down: 'Lootenant Groves, sir! Mister Martin was perfectly correct, sir,' stressing Josh's surname with particular relish. 'There is no sign of anyone else up there. Just a heap of broken adobe buildings!'

Then with mock formality he inquired: 'Permission to descend to terra firma, sir?' indicating that though currently a mere trooper, he was nevertheless a man of some education.

The lieutenant, irritated that he was being gently mocked and aware that he had made an error of judgement in not believing Josh and Ellie, replied in the affirmative: 'Yes, yes, Muller. Get down here and don't take all day about it!' And he turned away and stared long and hard across the valley, while Trooper Muller descended to the ground; here Muller was surrounded by his cheering comrades as he grasped Josh's right hand, shaking it up and down as though he were operating a water pump.

Muller then observed to the lieutenant: 'Lieutenant Groves, sir. This Mr Josh Martin and Miss Ellie both deserve medals in my opinion. They defended their position, and up there you can see where they tore down adobe walls to make ammunition for repelling their attackers, and you can see the results of their efforts all around us down here.' He pointed to the adobe-strewn surface upon which they were standing.

More composed, Lieutenant Groves thanked Trooper Muller for his report, and expressed an apology to Josh and Ellie; he then ordered the men to move to where the party attending the horses waited. With two of the troopers riding double, a mount was provided for Josh, who took Ellie behind him on the slow ride to the now partially dismantled Fort Emporium. A certain Trooper Marsh was sent ahead with a brief note to Lieutenant Groves' squadron commander, Major Smedley, informing him that the Casa Grande had been cleared of all inhabitants. Marsh, however, was bursting with the news of the two young people who had successfully held their ground against the Apache, and it is quite possible that the story became more than a trifle exaggerated by the time the rescue party, along with the two young heroes, arrived back at Fort Emporium and the military encampment.

Therefore Josh and Ellie were surprised to be met by large numbers of cheering civilians of both sexes, along with dozens of blue-clad troopers, who, choosing a suitable moment, pulled the startled boy and his female companion from the saddle. Hoisting them upon their shoulders, they bore the two triumphantly to the regimental headquarters where General Percivale was in conference with his staff and Diablito and the other chiefs. However, the uproar outside his headquarters irritated the general, and emerging and angrily calling for silence, he demanded the reason for the undisciplined behaviour.

Half-a-dozen voices all speaking at once answered his query, and Josh and Ellie were thrust forwards: they stood, inwardly quaking, before this bull of a man, invested with all the authority of the United States government.

The general stared at the young couple before him. He saw a rather grimy young man who had hurriedly snatched a battered hat from his head revealing a ragged mop of hair and several days' growth of fair whiskers. His apparel was more suited for a ragbag than as clothing: both shirt and jeans were rent and torn, and his appearance was hardly redeemed by the clean appearance of the heavy revolver hanging at his waist. His little companion was equally dirty and unkempt – her long hair had obviously not seen the attention of either comb or brush for several days, and her features, though comely, would most certainly profit from not merely a good wash but also a good scrubbing, as no doubt would the rest of her body. At

123

this point General Percivale hurriedly thrust from his mind the thought of this young woman standing naked before him in a tub of hot water.

He then recalled the adage drummed into him in his childhood, that 'cleanliness is next to godliness'. The two before him were dirty, therefore clearly ungodly, and he was filled with a sense of moral outrage. He declared: 'I can't speak to these people when they appear in this condition. Take them away and make them presentable, and then I may see them!' He turned away, leaving the small group of troopers standing amazed at their senior officer's apparently unjust dismissal of the two, while Josh and Ellie attempted to make sense of his attitude to them.

CHAPTER 21

A sergeant major came to their rescue. Handing over Ellie to one of the few respectable women in the enclosure, he hustled Josh away to a secluded area where he was stripped of his rags and made to stand in a piping hot tub of water; he was then soaped all over, and more thoroughly scrubbed than at any time since he was a small child. His repeated howls of protest fell on deaf ears as volunteers among the troopers worked on removing the accumulation of sweat, smoke stains and other indescribable dirt residues from Josh's body until he literally glowed.

Meanwhile, others had foraged around and obtained a shirt, jeans, men's drawers and socks to dress him in when finally he emerged from the torture of the tub. But before he could dress, he was handed over to the regimental barber, who shaved him expertly and cropped his unruly curls, while yet another trooper made a valiant effort to produce a modicum of a glow on Josh's battered boots.

While Josh was being restored to a civilized appearance, Ellie was undergoing very similar treatment. First she luxuriated in the pleasure of the hot tub and being washed gently all over with a delightful soap, the fragrance of which pervaded the whole tent where these ministrations occurred. Then her hair, after being towelled relatively dry, was vigorously brushed and gathered into a single pigtail secured with pink ribbon. Finally she was permitted to dress in clean under-things, including a white chemise and modestly frilly under-drawers. Of socks there were none available, but the ladies present thought that would be all right with her brown, suntanned legs and ankles. A long dress had been found: when Ellie put it on, it came down to her ankles, and it felt so different and restraining compared to the clothes she was used to. No suitable footwear could be obtained, but Ellie was furnished with a pair of women's beaded moccasins provided by one of the troopers. The last item she put on was the holster containing the Smith and Wesson that Josh had handed to her. It was a trifle incongruous, but not out of place, given the prevailing circumstances.

At last the pair of them were considered suitably clean and presentable to appear before General Percivale, and they were escorted to the tent where the senior officers were still in conference. Curiously, the pair of young people were strangely shy when they were brought together after being cleansed and re-clothed. After days of very close, grubby companionship, the transformation was startling for both of them.

Ellie looked at Josh and saw a well built young man smiling shyly at her, and a total stranger in his new clothing. In fact the only thing about Josh that she recognized was his gun-belt and the revolver that he had removed from one of the men who had tried to molest her. Josh, for his part, was totally embarrassed by the sight of the comely young woman standing before him, so far removed from the dirty, smoke-stained ragamuffin who had cuddled up to him every night from the time when he had discovered her cowering in the cave after the torture and death of those whom she had thought of as almost her parents.

Both were tongue-tied, but soon attempted to break down the barrier that had risen between them as they waited for permission to have an audience with the general. First, Josh burst out with: 'Gee, Ellie! You sure are looking fine in them new duds. Though better take them off before you do any cooking or fire making!' He stopped in confusion, turning red at the implication of his remark. 'I mean, you'd have to wear something else when you were working!'

Ellie smiled sweetly at her companion and thanked him for the compliment, remarking: 'You know Josh, underneath all that dirt and grime there's quite a good-looking fella. You really do look quite handsome! You'll be sparking up to all the girls in future!'

Their interchange was interrupted by an orderly, who took them into the general's tent: here they stood, overawed by the officers who sat staring at them, while Diablito and his chiefs stood impassively with their armed folded. The transformation in the young couple's appearance was too much for the sluggish thought process of General Percivale, and he regarded them owlishly – finally it was Diablito who broke the silence.

Standing, the Apache chief advanced on the two young White Eyes, saying: 'It is a great honour for me, Diablito, to greet the two young warriors who fought against The People with such cunning and bravery.' So saying, he took a necklace of bear claws from around his neck, and draped it over that of Josh; and removing a silver bracelet from his left wrist, he placed this on Ellie's quivering arm. Poor Ellie wasn't sure how to react to this unexpected gift. She had shrunk back against Josh as the Indian approached, but seeing him smile, she looked down at the silver adorning her wrist, and curtsied most gracefully. Simultaneously, both of them uttered words of thanks to Diablito, as the Apache chief, holding them both by the arm, declared that they would always be welcome in his wickiup.

General Percivale, not to be outdone by these displays of generosity, replaced the scowl on his florid features with a fixed smile of pleasure, and bustled forwards, uttering the first thing that entered his mind: 'Well done, young fella! Splendid work, eh!' Then, mixing up his wars, he continued, 'Really got the damned Johnny Rebels on the run this time – well done! Give me your hand!' and he started pumping Josh's arm up and down while at the same time he ogled Ellie.

Finally getting his military situations sorted out in his mind, he turned to where the regimental officers sat bemused by the general's antics, and declared: 'Smedley! Arrange for two extra places at the regimental dinner this evening. We must all learn the details of the exploits these young people have been engaged in!'

Thus Josh and Ellie, along with Diablito and two of his chiefs, were the guests of honour at a dinner in the military camp set up beside the dismantled Fort Emporium. Apart from confusion over the array of silverware that lay beside each dinner plate, the pair of them managed quite well; they were seated one each side of General Percivale and across from Diablito, who was equally unsure about which of the multiple knives and forks he should use as the various dishes were brought to the table.

As the dinner progressed, Josh, encouraged by the general and by other officers, told his story of the wrecked stagecoach, the discovery of Ellie, and their subsequent experiences with the Apache Gray Hawk and the white men whom they encountered. He described in more detail how they decided to climb up to the adobes of Casa Grande as a safe place of refuge, and the attempts of various warriors to breach their defences. While giving his account of dropping adobe bricks on to the ascending Apaches he glanced at Diablito and shrugged apologetically – and was relieved when Diablito burst out laughing at the thought of seasoned warriors being defeated by a stream of bricks originally created by their own ancestors.

Ellie, meanwhile, though enjoying both the food and the attentions paid to her by various young officers, was also fighting a silent battle of her own, as periodically, General Percivale's right hand would drop from the table on to her left leg. Initially it appeared so casual and accidental that she ignored it, but that would seem to have encouraged the amorous old man, as the hand appeared once more and started sliding gently up and down with the occasional squeeze. Firmly, she then lifted his hand and removed it from her leg, while at the same time smiling sweetly at a young captain who had just given her a compliment.

Once more the hand rested upon her leg and started exploring upwards, and Ellie decided that it was time to make a counter attack. Picking up her dinner fork she deliberately fumbled it and dropped it towards her lap, catching it before the tines touched her dress. Then she jabbed firmly at the pudgy hand on her thigh. There was an audible 'Ouch!' from the pain-stricken general as he suddenly withdrew the injured member and sucked at the four puncture wounds in the back of his hand. He looked at Ellie reproachfully and was singularly silent for the remainder of the meal, while around him the others present were seen to be enjoying both the dinner and the company present.

CHAPTER 22

While the regimental dinner was proceeding, an important discussion regarding a particular economic situation was taking place a couple of hundred yards away. There were only two people involved, but they were discussing the dire downturn of their financial profits due to the recent siege and its outcome.

One of the participants was Mother Carey, the madam and ostensible owner of the brothel, which had sprung into being shortly after the first miners had arrived in the valley of the Casa Grande. Her sleeping partner – in a financial sense that is, since the mere thought of coupling with the fat old woman was enough to create in him a feeling of revulsion – was Snake Dakota. Still, business is business!

Snake was a gambler, and was known far and wide for offering a moderately square game, though men in the know were aware that, given the opportunity to fleece a greenhorn, he would not pass the prospect by, even if it meant dealing from the bottom of the deck. However, few people knew that Snake was a 50 per cent partner in Mother Carey's flesh enterprise, and he was content to leave it that way, as long as his half of the profits were turned over to him on a regular basis.

And therein lay the problem, resulting in their evening conference. Mother Carey was explaining, 'Like any business Snake, there are several reasons why our take has bin less recently. The siege has meant that most of the menfolk here have bin so busy at the barricades that, when they've bin relieved from duty, they've just wanted to sleep, regardless of where or who they're with. That's one factor. Then there's the girls. I've bin short staffed for weeks now. You know we lost Elsie. The damned little fool would go and stick her head up to see what was going on. Got an arrow right in the throat. That stopped her squealing!

'Then there was Tommy. You know, Tomasina. Pretty little thing. Always good for a full night's work. Suddenly, in the middle of the siege, she gets religion. Decided that she didn't want to be the "whore of Babylon", nor of any other berg. And if that wasn't enough, she takes up with that psalm-singing teamster Alf Collins – you know, the one with the big muscles. Got married all respectable like, dang blast her!'

Snake looked at her sympathetically, shaking his head at the thought of these young girls who showed such ingratitude after having been given a good home. 'Well, m'dear, you'll just have to get some new fillies in your stable to replace your losses.'

Mother Carey spread her hands wide. 'And how can I do that, stuck in this God-forsaken hole – and just when it was beginning to pay, being kicked out by the bloomin' army! It's not as though we're in a place like Santa Fe where you can pick up likely girls on the street. But here?' She shook her head in disgust.

The gambler commiserated with her, and then a thought struck him: 'I say! What about that girl the troopers brought in today? As I understand she has neither kith nor kin anywhere in the world, and the only friend that she appears to have is that boy who apparently was with her up in the Casa Grande. Clean her up! Sell her your usual story, and you'll have one more girl, I'll be bound!' Snake sat back with a complacent air at having partially solved Mother Carey's problem.

Her eyes brightened, and a wide smile appeared on her face revealing broken and discoloured teeth. 'Now, there's a possible solution, Snake! Why didn't I think of that? I'll get on to it right away, jus' leave it to me!' – and with that remark the economic conference was brought to a close.

CHAPTER 23

Back at the regimental dinner Ellie was quite frankly getting more than a little bored. General Percivale pointedly ignored her after her successful counter attack, and just sat and periodically sucked the back of his right hand, while Ellie listened to the polite inane comments made by the more junior members at the dinner. Finally Major Smedley, noticing her boredom, kindly suggested that perhaps she might wish to withdraw, as was the usual custom for ladies at such dinners – at which notion Ellie thankfully rose; leaving Josh in animated conversation with an unknown captain, she thanked the general, her host, and requested permission to depart.

General Percivale muttered a gruff, 'Thank you for coming, m'dear!' and Ellie departed, declining the many escort offerings on the part of some of the junior officers. 'No thank you, gentlemen! It is but a short distance and still light. I'll be perfectly all right.' So saying, she stepped outside, and passing the armed guard, who brought his carbine to the salute position, she walked towards the encampment.

At that moment Ellie heard the sound of a girl crying off to the left in the gloom of the deepening shadows. This aroused her curiosity, and she turned to discover the source of the noise – and found a slightly built girl crouched amidst a number of bales and barrels sobbing, with both hands covering her face.

Ellie approached her and placed one hand gently on the girl's shoulder. 'What's the problem, dear? Can I help you?'

The unknown girl lowered her hands following Ellie's inquiry, revealing a tear-stained face with eyes red from crying. She grabbed Ellie's hand and pressed it to her cheek. 'Oh, please would you help me find the brooch?' She went on amid sobs and sniffs to describe how she had taken, without permission, her mother's heirloom brooch and had somehow lost it. When she had confessed to the crime her mother had sent her out to look for the missing jewellery with the warning not to come home without it!

To Ellie it sounded as though Freda – for that was the girl's name – was terrified of her mother, and she willingly volunteered to assist in the search for the missing brooch. She took hold of Freda's right hand and pulled her up from her crouched position. 'Come on, I'll help you look for it. Two pairs of eyes are better than one!' And hand in hand the girls wandered among the debris of the dismantled camp seeking the missing brooch.

But in fact Freda had the missing item concealed in her left hand, and dropped it as they wandered slowly among the discarded packing cases and broken barrels that littered the area. Having found nothing, at Freda's suggestion they retraced their footsteps with their eyes still searching diligently as they progressed. It appeared to be purely by luck that Ellie suddenly saw something glinting in the moonlight, and swooping down, triumphantly seized the missing brooch, declaring: 'Here it is, Freda! Now you can go home, and I'm sure your ma will just be happy that you found her jewellery!'

Freda took the brooch and gave Ellie a big hug. 'Oh, you're so kind to me, a total stranger. Will you do one thing more? Come and tell my mother how her brooch was found, so she will understand. I'm sure she'll be pleased to see you!'

Ellie hesitated, and then, thinking that she needn't stay long, agreed to go with Freda. So hand in hand the two girls went the short distance to the edge of the encampment where there stood a large covered wagon with light shining through the canvas tilt. Freda mounted the wooden steps at the rear of the wagon and tapped nervously on the canvas. 'It's me, Mamma, Freda! We've found your brooch. I've got a friend I'd like you to meet. May we come in?'

There was the sound of someone untying the laces that secured the end flaps of the wagon, and an older woman appeared, declaring 'Freda, dearest! I wasn't worried about that old brooch, sweetheart, but you found it anyway. Certainly you can bring your friend. Come up, the pair of you!' A plump white arm held the flap open wide, while a heavily ring-adorned hand beckoned the two girls to enter her abode.

Freda looked down at Ellie and said: 'Come on, Ellie. My mother will certainly be pleased to meet you!' and Ellie hesitantly, yet with the curiosity of her sex, climbed up the steps and entered the wagon. The interior, though space was limited, was lavishly equipped with a large single bed along the right side with a satin-covered eiderdown and snowy white sheets. On the left was a built-in couch and a dressing table on which were strewn a number of bottles and glasses.

The sole occupant of the wagon was Freda's mother. She was a large woman with a mass of obviously dyed blonde hair piled on the top of her head. She smiled a welcome at Ellie, revealing a number of discoloured teeth, and a mouth with rouge-applied lips. Her ample body was encased in a house wrap of startling colours, and from the bottom of this voluminous garment peeked a pair of ridiculously impractical pink slippers. But despite her rather bizarre appearance she extended a warm welcome to Ellie.

'Ellie, my dear. I'm so pleased to meet you. Come and sit down here. . .' she said, patting the couch with her left hand '. . . and we'll have a nice little chat.'

A trifle reluctantly Ellie responded to the invitation, and sank down on the couch, wishing that she had stayed at the dinner. To Freda's mother she gave a series of short muttered replies in answer to the many queries the older woman fired at her, and then without being impolite, indicated that she should be leaving.

'Yes dear, it is getting late. I'll tell you what – how

about a small glass of cordial before you go? It's hardly alcoholic. I've never approved of young ladies imbibing strong liquors.' So saying, she turned to her dressing table and poured three glasses of a pale amber liquid from a green bottle, handing one to Freda and one to Ellie while retaining one for herself.

'There you are, Ellie. Just a pleasant way to end an evening. Here's to your good health!' And she raised her glass and tossed the contents into her mouth with a hearty sigh of contentment. Freda did likewise, and Ellie, not to be left out, also swallowed her glassful of cordial.

The liquid was pleasant to the taste, and swallowing it she felt a warm glow as it went down to her stomach. But shortly thereafter she began to feel strangely listless, and had great difficulty in keeping her eyes open. When Freda's mother spoke to her, her voice seemed to be coming from a great distance away – and then both women in the wagon appeared to be advancing and receding in her vision, until finally Ellie slumped over on the couch, unconscious from the Mickey Finn that Mother Carey had artfully administered to her.

Swiftly Mother Carey turned to Freda: 'Quickly now girl! Get that dress off her and help me secure her while she's having her beauty sleep. Make haste now!'

Between them the two women divested Ellie of the dress she had been given upon reaching Fort Emporium, and tying her hands together, fastened them to the head of the bed; likewise they secured her feet to the foot of the bed, then gagged her, and for full measure, fastened a blindfold over her eyes.

Seeing Freda admiring the bracelet Ellie was wearing, her 'mother' stated; 'Yes, you may take it, but don't flash it around. Now go and join the other girls. They'll be leaving later. Now off with you!'

Freda left, and Mother Carey sat back with a satisfied sigh. Then she called out to her waiting teamster: 'OK, Bill! Let's get this wagon on the road! With a full moon you should have no trouble!' And lurching and swaying from side to side, the heavy vehicle rolled slowly away from the encampment.

CHAPTER 24

Josh had been getting more and more worried. During the regimental dinner he had noticed Ellie's look of boredom and was therefore not too concerned when she rose and asked to be excused – after all, that was what ladies did at such functions, or so Josh thought. So Ellie left, and Josh continued the lively conversation that he was having with several of the younger officers present. It was therefore much later in the evening when he, too, departed and made his way to the quarters they had been assigned. But to his surprise Ellie wasn't there, and a number of inquiries of neighbours produced negative responses.

Over in the Apache encampment there was some kind of jubilation taking place, with tribal dancing amid the solemn beating of drums. Had Ellie's curiosity taken her in that direction? Or – and a horrible thought struck Josh – had she been kidnapped by some warrior who fancied the notion of having a white girl as his squaw? As Josh set off with determined gait to the Apache camp he gave scarce notice to the large wagon leaving the dismantled Fort Emporium, merely giving the teamster a disinterested wave as the former offered him a cheery 'Good evening!'

At the Apache camp the repeated showing of the bear-claw necklace gained him an audience with Diablito, who was sitting with the other chiefs enjoying the celebrations. After being greeted effusively by the chief and acknowledged by all those seated, Josh explained the reason for his visit, and diplomatically explained his suspicions that Ellie might be with some amorous brave.

Diablito's bronzed features grew stern, and he burst into a staccato stream of the Apache language, which sent warriors hunting all over the camp to ensure that none were hiding the missing white girl. One by one the searchers returned with negative results, and Josh must have shown his dismay since Diablito clapped him on the shoulder saying; 'Be of good heart, my young friend! We will find the one that you call Ellie. I, Diablito, am also concerned that the little female warrior is missing. There may be a simple reason for her disappearance, but we must make sure. The People will help you in your search!'

He called out for a particular warrior to come forwards, and introduced him to Josh. 'This is Red Fox: he is of my family. Actually, you two have met before, but at that time you were above and he was below!'

Diablito noted the uncomfortable look on Josh's face, and hastened to assure the white boy that Red Fox bore him no ill will. He nodded to the young Apache warrior, who introduced himself in broken

English: 'Josh, Adobe warrior. I, Red Fox, happy to work with you to find Ellie the female warrior!' – and he stuck out his right hand in friendship. Josh was pleased to respond, and they shook hands, both as a token of friendship and as a pact to search for the missing one.

Together the two young men, with Red Fox leading his Indian pony, walked back to the dismantled fort, where Josh outlined what he had done to date to locate Ellie. The problem was that trying to trace the girl's tracks was well nigh impossible with the ground scuffed by the passage of many feet, and the fact that despite the presence of a bright full moon, much of the camp-site remained in deep shadow. Reluctantly it was decided to call off the search until daylight, and therefore Josh took Red Fox to his quarters to rest, despite the strange looks from the white folks in the area.

In the morning both young men searched diligently all over the area once more, and Josh spread the word regarding Ellie's disappearance. There was no sign of the girl, and Josh became more than desperate: he felt frantic at the way Ellie had vanished without a trace. It was just as though she had never existed.

The pair of searchers were standing close to the area where they had spent the night. Josh was completely disconsolate, while Red Fox, with the persistence of his race, stood motionless while his eyes continued to scan the scene before him, noting every detail of each activity, and each passerby as they entered his vision. Then suddenly he moved, grabbing Josh's arm in a vice-like grip: 'Josh look! See young squaw with straw hair. Look at squaw's arm. She has Diablito's gift to Ellie!'

Josh stared in the direction that the young Apache warrior indicated. Sure enough, there was a young woman sauntering past with her eyes firmly fixed upon a group of off-duty troopers who were just idly taking in the activities around them.

Although it was early in the day, Freda was always ready to ply her trade, and had issued forth that morning fully prepared to offer her services to any soldier or civilian desiring a quick tumble. As she had been finishing her toilette after breaking her fast, her eyes had settled upon the silver bracelet that Ma had generously bestowed upon her, and she could not resist wearing it to flaunt before the other girls and also to enhance her considerable charms to any potential client.

Freda walked slowly past the troopers, swaying her hips provocatively, and with a fixed professional smile on her ruby-painted lips, deliberately ignored the wolf whistles and comments that were coming in her direction. She was very familiar with the admiration of menfolk that was thrown her way, and so was not at all surprised when she heard footsteps hurrying behind her: a strong hand grasped her elbow and a male voice declared: 'Let's you and I go somewhere quiet an' just have a little talk, shall we?'

She turned her head and glanced, smiling, at the young civilian who had chosen to walk with her – and mentally Freda dismissed the troopers as potential customers as she noted the manner of his dress, from the

clean apparel to the big pistol swinging at his hip.
'Hmm. This bird has money, I'll be bound! Well,
maybe I can pluck him of some, or all of it.'

They strolled to a small lean-to draped with canvas
where Freda had plied her trade for several weeks, and
opening the entrance flap, she bade him enter. The
young man did so – and suddenly Freda's world came
crashing down about her ears. He grabbed her around
the waist with his left arm, while the fingers of his right
hand seized her by the throat, squeezing gently and
forcing her head back to prevent her from screaming.

He called out softly; 'OK, Red Fox, come in and
guard the entrance!' and to Freda's absolute terror a
young Apache brave entered her lean-to and stood
there with arms folded, staring impassively at her. The
young man looked at the young whore with loathing,
and said grimly: 'I'm going to ask you some questions,
and you are going to answer them truthfully. And if
you don't, I'll turn you over to my friend here. Now,
first, your name?' He eased the grip on her throat to
permit her half-strangled answer: 'Freda.'

'OK, Freda! Very good. Now! The silver bracelet
that you are wearing: where did you get it from?'

Freda liked the bracelet and desperately decided to
fabricate a story to explain her possession of the
trinket: 'My Ma gave it to me as a present when I left
home, honestly!'

Josh removed the bracelet from her arm, and slipping it into a pocket, looked at her in disgust. 'You lie,
Freda! Now you tell me the absolute truth about the
bracelet, and what has happened to the girl who was

wearing it yesterday, or I am going to turn the questioning over to my Apache friend here. How would you like to have a dirty nose treatment?' and Josh spent a few moments explaining how unfaithful Indian women had their noses slit as an outward sign of their adultery. 'How would that improve your looks, Freda? I fear you wouldn't draw many customers!' and Josh forced her head to look at Red Fox who had drawn a glittering knife and was standing with a look of anticipation, honing the blade on the palm of his hand.

It was too much for Freda, and a pool of water gathered at her feet. 'Keep him away from me, Mister! I'll tell you everything!' Josh relaxed his grip on her throat, and nodded for her to continue. Freda did so, describing how Mother Carey had planned to obtain yet another girl for her brothel, and how they had enticed Ellie into the trap prepared for her. Josh was horrified when he realized that he had been but a couple of yards away from the wagon in which Ellie was confined, and in fact had waved to the teamster who was no doubt in league with Mother Carey.

Freda was by now so anxious to redeem herself in the eyes of Josh and his terrible Apache friend that she gladly revealed the route to be taken by the Carey wagon, and which the remaining girls were to follow; she also revealed the house that was their destination in Santa Fe. There was one further piece of news that Freda offered as proof of her sincerity, namely, that Mother Carey had a silent partner who apparently had the controlling say in all that the brothel madam did, and who undoubtedly would have suggested the abduction of Ellie as a way of increasing the bawdy house membership.

'Never met him!' volunteered Freda, '. . .'cos I came from another house, but I understand that the new girls were terrified of him. They say that he boasted that a new girl was like a wild horse and had to be whipped to do as she was told. They say he's a real devil!'

Josh was filled with a wild anger at the thought that Ellie was in such a perilous situation, at least partly because of the girl he now held, and he instinctively tightened his grip upon her.

'What's the name of Mother Carey's partner? Quickly now, or by God I'll turn you over to the Apaches for treatment!' – and he swung her in the direction of the waiting Red Fox.

Terrified, Freda blurted out the name of Snake Dakota, and said that he was a gambler, and that she believed he was still in Fort Emporium. Josh then eased her down upon her cot, and with a dire warning not to say a word of what had happened that evening, he and his Apache friend left the lean-to.

Josh walked around the enclosure speaking to various troopers and civilians whom he had met in the short time since they had left the Casa Grande. He told of Ellie's abduction and of the suspected part played by Snake Dakota, who already had an unsavory reputation in the camp as a man who was believed to deal from the bottom of a deck of cards, though nobody had been able to prove that such was the case.

146

Josh had a purpose in stating his case. He knew that he had to go after Ellie, but he also wanted Snake detained, to prevent him from following the wagon and also to ensure that in some way he paid for what he was doing to young girls such as Ellie.

CHAPTER 25

The constant jolting of the wagon wheels over the rough terrain had woken Ellie from her drugged sleep hours earlier. Being blindfolded and bound hand and foot, in addition to having a gag in her mouth, meant that the only sensations she could experience was the hearing of the horses clip-clopping along the rocky trail and the pressure her body felt as the vehicle lurched in its progress from the valley.

Slowly Ellie tried to assemble her jumbled thoughts into some kind of order. She realized very quickly that Freda's plight had been nothing but a sham, a device to get her into the wagon in which she was now travelling. But why? Why would anyone wish to kidnap a young penniless girl for whom there was no possibility of ransom?

Was it possible that the two females, Freda and her mother, intended to sell their victim into bondage, possibly to the Mormons, about whom she had heard many strange stories? Ellie had also heard of girls being kidnapped and smuggled down into Mexico, where they survived as slaves on isolated haciendas. She shivered at the thought of such an existence. The single thought that flashed through her mind was: 'Oh Josh! Where are you?'

Josh had spent an anxious day searching for Ellie, first interrogating Freda and then enlisting allies in the form of troopers and various civilians to aid him by detaining Snake Dakota. After a restless night he was now ready to hit the trail together with Red Fox in search of Mother Carey's wagon. With a borrowed horse and the Apache's Indian pony, the pair set out in the early morning as the sun just started to peer shyly over the mountains to the east. They left behind a self-appointed posse of vigilantes determined to locate the crooked gambler who had connived with Mother Carey to steal Ellie, the young heroine of the siege of the ruins of Casa Grande.

Teamsters had assured Josh that the heavy wagon drawn by mules would have not travelled too far in the time since it had left Fort Emporium, and would not have reached Fort Burnside. Said one: 'If Bill Gates is driving that there wagon, an' I'd bet my last dollar he is, those mules will have to be given a decent rest every few hours or he'll have dead animals dropping in the traces.' Other teamsters agreed with the bearded one's analysis, and Josh was reassured by the thought that at some time in the coming hours they would catch up with the fleeing wagon, and that he would rescue Ellie.

*

Ellie felt hands fumbling around her head, and suddenly the blindfold cloth was removed and she was forced to shut her eyes tightly against the glare of the sunlight penetrating the canvas tilt of the wagon. Slowly she reopened her eyes and, squinting, was able turn her head and survey the interior of her prison.

There was only one other person present, and Ellie wondered what had become of Freda. The ample figure of Mother Carey stared down at her with a grim, self-satisfied smile on her rouge-caked features.

'Well, young Ellie! I think that you and I are going to have a little talk about your future, and depending what comes out of our chat, I might release your bonds or at least remove that gag. Now, what I'm going to tell you is actually for your own good, so listen carefully, my girl!

'I am what is called a "Madam". That is, I own a house of pleasure in Santa Fe where gentlemen come to, ah, shall we say relieve themselves of all the pressures that they have accumulated during the day. My young ladies are trained to entertain our male visitors in many ways, and, though I say it myself, we have a reputation of being the best establishment in the city.

'When you become one of my young ladies you are being given a chance to be recognized as somebody special. You will have a room of your own. You'll wear the finest clothes including silk underthings, and the best dresses money can buy, and will be waited on hand and foot.

'I know that you must be startled at the manner in which you were taken, but I was in a hurry to get back to Santa Fe and decided that we could come to an arrangement on the way.

'Now, later today a gentleman will be coming to see you when my mules stop for a rest. If you are sensible you will cooperate and give yourself to him without any fuss, but I must warn you this man carries a dog whip and is not averse to using it on any foolish woman who thwarts his desires. So, it's up to you my girl. Is it to be pain or pleasure? The choice is yours!'

From Mother Carey's viewpoint once a girl had, like a young colt, been thoroughly broken in, generally there was no going back. They believed that they were, as described, 'soiled doves', and that few decent men would associate with them, and so they accepted their lot.

Ellie had listened to Mother Carey's calm determination to change her into a common whore with horror and disgust, and made a secret vow to herself that she would not let the described fate happen to her. Meanwhile, she decided that all she could do for the moment was to play along with the wicked old woman and wait for an opportunity to make a bid for freedom.

So, when Carey leaned forward and asked, 'Ellie, are you going to shout out and make a fuss or start screaming if I remove your gag?' Ellie closed her eyes and shook her head slowly from side to side, whereupon the gag was removed. Her mouth felt dry and her tongue thick, and Ellie licked her lips and asked 'Do you think that I could have a little water, please?'

Mother Carey, pleased that her captive was so

docile, hastened to answer the girl's request, and pouring water into a glass, she lifted Ellie's head and placed the container to her lips and allowed a trickle of the life fluid into Ellie's mouth. Ellie gulped the water down her throat, and looked pleadingly for more.

The thoughts of the two people inside the wagon at that moment were in total opposition to the other. Ellie was thinking that given the slightest chance she would free herself and make a bid for freedom, even if it meant overcoming Mother Carey by force. She also knew in her heart that Josh would have been searching for her for some time now, and at that very moment might be following the trail of the missing wagon. A thought struck her.

'I say! Where's that girl Freda who took me to your wagon? I don't see her around here anywhere?'

'Don't you worry your head about her, Ellie. She's stayed behind with the other ladies, but they'll all be along shortly.'

She was confident that the other girls were sufficiently well trained that they would obey her instructions implicitly, and would leave the mining camp quietly and without the fanfares that were normally employed to announce their arrivals and departures. Mother Carey was also becoming concerned at the continued absence of Snake Dakota. Their original plan was that he would leave the camp early in the morning after the wagon left the night before. That would give him plenty of time to indulge in his 'training session' with the new girl before they reached Santa Fe. Where could that man have got to? Probably heavy into a game of cards and, having a winning streak, he can't let go. Damn him!

CHAPTER 26

Snake Dakota wasn't on a winning streak – in fact he wasn't playing anything, though no doubt he was damned. Snake, with his hands tied behind his back, was turning slowly round and round with his head twisted at an unnatural angle and his tongue protruding in a most unseemly way from a blackened face. There was absolutely no doubt about it: Snake Dakota was well and truly dead!

Earlier the vigilante posse had set out to comb the camp looking for Snake, when one of the miners observed that the gambler was no doubt in his usual place of business, namely the tented establishment, The Lucky Nugget. So the self-appointed body of law and order, plus two or three dozen hangers-on, went to the saloon to arrest Snake Dakota.

The gambler was deep into a lengthy game of poker, and all his powers of concentration were upon the cards. When the crowd of vigilantes et al appeared with cries of 'There he is! There's Snake! Don't let him get away! Grab him boys!' Snake lost his head completely. He rose to his feet drawing a .38 calibre Smith and Wesson revolver from a shoulder holster as he did so. One of the crowd picked up a bottle from a nearby table and threw it at Snake's gun arm, missed, and hit one of the card players in the face. Snake turned and fired wildly, missing the bottle thrower but sadly hitting one of the saloon girls in the head and killing her instantly.

The crowd howled with anger, and before Snake could fire another shot he was seized amid cries of 'Bloody murderer! Woman killer! String him up!' And since the last statement was by far the most popular, they proceeded to do just that.

One of the huge tent poles that supported the canvas of the marquee had a short cross piece from which could be hung additional lighting, and thus created a convenient gallows. Snake was hustled and jostled over to the tent pole, his hands ruthlessly tied behind his back and a noose hung around his neck. Then he was lifted up on to a chair where he stood quivering while the crowd waited to see if he had any memorable last words.

None were forthcoming, and someone kicked the chair away from under him. Snake hung there choking with his legs drawn up spasmodically as he attempted wildly to avoid being strangled. His efforts were in vain, and finally the struggles ended and his lifeless body swung gently back and forth against the tent pole, while the crowd, subdued by the sight of death, dispersed and went their various ways.

CHAPTER 27

Josh and Red Fox rode along the trail in easy companionship, neither needing to break the silence that existed between them. The Apache warrior was thinking of a young squaw, Morning Sunlight, who always smiled at him as she passed by intent on some of her womanish duties. She was very pleasing to look at, and Red Fox was mentally counting up his assets and wondering if he had reached the state of life where he should consider having a woman, and whether her father would demand many horses if he, Red Fox, were to ask for his daughter.

Josh, too, was thinking of the opposite sex in the form of Ellie. Her prolonged absence had really played upon him, and the fact that he missed her so sorely bothered him, and convinced him more than ever on the need not merely to rescue her for her sake, but to have her close once more. He thought back to the days when they were alone, making their way towards the settlement, and realized that despite their privations there had been something idyllic in the situation. When I rescue Ellie I'm going to ask her to marry me, he decided, as he and the Apache rode along.

At last in the far distance they could see a covered wagon drawn up on the left side of the trail close to a high wall of rock. Behind the wagon and thus closer to them could be seen the figure of a man, presumably the teamster, stretched out in the shade taking advantage of the halt to obtain a little shut-eye.

Inside the wagon Mother Carey was getting increasingly concerned at the prolonged absence of her partner Snake Dakota. 'Dang blast the man! What the hell is he doing!' Due to the circumstances she was still dressed in the frilly lace-adorned housecoat of the previous evening with the ridiculous fur-trimmed pink slippers, and so she could hardly leave the wagon even to just peer up the trail.

Though hardly dressed for even the slightest form of manual labour, Mother Carey decided that she had to do something to keep her mind occupied. But what? One little job that needed doing was that of filling the two large kerosene lamps used at night-time to produce both light and warmth inside the wagon. Setting the two lamps upon her dressing table, she removed the filler caps and, reaching down, lifted up the gallon can of kerosene oil. Momentarily the screwed top stuck and she wrestled with it, watched by an alert Ellie through half-closed eyes. The top came free suddenly, and Mother Carey spilled a considerable quantity of vile-reeking oil on the floor before she succeeded in filling one of the lamps.

There was some kind of disturbance outside, and she lowered the can to the floor and picked up Ellie's pistol from her dressing table where it had lain since she and Freda had removed it from the girl's unconscious body the night before. Drawing the revolver from its holster, she waited with the gun held down at her side concealed by her gown.

Down the trail on the Casa Grande side Josh and Red Fox had quietly dismounted, and leaving their mounts secured to some convenient mesquite bushes, had walked slowly, with pistols drawn, up to the dozing teamster. Bill Gates, deep in slumber where he was engaged in frivolous love play in a dream world of his own, was suddenly rudely awakened. The hard, callous hand of Red Fox covered Gates' mouth, while a second grasped him by the throat, and simultaneously, the muzzle of a large pistol was pressed against his temple by Josh. He distinctly heard the action cocked as a voice in English whispered: 'Not a word out of you!' The gun pressed harder: 'Not a single squeak, d'you hear?' Gates carefully nodded to his captors that indeed he would be more silent than a church mouse.

'Now! Who's in the wagon?' The teamster responded that as far as he knew, by all the saints in heaven, there was just Mother Carey and a single girl she had picked up in the camp. He, Bill Gates, didn't know anything about it – he just drove the wagon. Nobody ever told him nothing. Ignoring his mangled use of the English tongue, he was gagged and tied up firmly with his own bootlaces; then, leaving Red Fox to guard the prisoner, Josh crept to the rear of the wagon and silently mounted the steps.

As he reached the top step, a brassy female voice challenged him from inside: 'I don't know who you are out there, but get away from here! I mean it!' Then, with more than a slight exaggeration, she continued: 'I've got a shotgun loaded with buckshot waiting for the first person who comes through that wagon flap!'

This was where Ellie, though tied up, played a hand, calling out, 'Don't believe her, whoever you are! She's got no shotgun. Just a little pistol she stole from me!' And Josh, upon hearing Ellie's voice, slashed at the strings holding the end flaps and stepped into the wagon. In a trice he had stepped to her side, and cutting the bonds tying her to both ends of the bed, he gathered her in his arms. Mother Carey, enraged at seeing her new asset vanishing before her eyes, cocked the Smith and Wesson before swinging it up to shoot Josh in the back.

However, things didn't work out quite the way she intended. Having never fired this pistol before, she was not aware that it had a sensitive filed action and therefore the gun was still pointed at the floor of the wagon when she applied but a light pressure on the trigger. The gun fired. The floor with its strip of brocaded carpet had been liberally dosed with kerosene spilled from the can, and when this received the long muzzle flash from the Smith and Wesson the results were disastrous. The carpet burst into flame, which quickly caught the edge of her gown alight. Mother

Carey swung round terrified, and in doing so knocked the can of kerosene to the floor, adding to the conflagration.

Josh, with Ellie in his arms, jumped to the ground and carried his precious burden well clear of the burning wagon before returning to try and save Mother Carey. It was far too late. The sun-bleached parts of the wagon, laced with the spilled oil, burned merrily, accompanied by the despairing shrieks of the woman, by now engulfed by the flames. She was like a living torch – all of her clothing and hair were now on fire, as were her surroundings. There was nothing to be done to save her, and Ellie, staring at the awful sight, pleaded with Josh: 'Please Josh! Shoot her! End this terrible sight!' Josh reluctantly drew his Remington revolver and, sighting carefully, sent a .44 calibre bullet into the head of the tortured being before him, thus ending her earthly misery.

There is not much to add to end this story. The mules were saved and set free, and Bill Gates was freed and permitted to depart, a poorer and wiser man. Red Fox returned to his people, having made vows of eternal friendship with both Ellie and Josh, and that couple, finally together and free of the Casa Grande, made their way to Fort Burnside. Here they found a minister who presided over a marriage where they swore to remain faithful to each other for the whole of their earthly existence. Let us hope that they were!